P9-DYD-257

Eden in the desert

"There has been no crime in Quenan for fifty years," the Teacher said. Ellery, looking around the lush, hidden valley, at the Quenanites contentedly working at their appointed tasks, could believe that; the close-knit, unworldly community was insulated from need and stress, and wisely led. Yet *someone* had made a duplicate key to the sanctum where Quenan's ancient treasure was stored.

And Ellery knew that the key would be used—that crime would return to the community that night, and that Quenan's innocence would be lost forever. . . .

Other titles by Ellery Queen on the
Ballantine Books list:

DOUBLE, DOUBLE
THE PLAYER ON THE OTHER SIDE
THE MURDERER IS A FOX

available at your local bookstore

And on the Eighth Day

Ellery Queen

BALLANTINE BOOKS • NEW YORK

© Copyright, 1964, by Ellery Queen

All rights reserved under International and
Pan-American Copyright Conventions.

Library of Congress Catalog Card Number: 64-10536

SBN 345-24552-0-125

This edition published by arrangement with
Random House, Inc.

First Printing: August, 1975

Printed in the United States of America

BALLANTINE BOOKS
A Division of Random House, Inc.
201 East 50th Street, New York, N.Y. 10022
Simultaneously published by
Ballantine Books, Ltd., Toronto, Canada

CONTENTS

I

SUNDAY

April 2.

SOMEWHERE SAGEBRUSH WAS burning, but on neither side of the road could Ellery see smoke. Once he thought he saw fire. It turned out to be an ocotillo shrub in flaming flower. Either the spring rains had fallen earlier than usual, or the elevation in this part of the desert brought occasional rainfall throughout the year.

He decided it was a campfire, perhaps from a wish. He had run across no human trail for hours, except the road itself.

A fuzzy whim had made him turn off into the state road east of Hamlin (named, a sun-roasted marker said, after Lincoln's first Vice-President). The road had been passable as far as it went; the trouble was, it had not gone far enough. About fifty miles from Hamlin it suddenly became an untidy wound. The California highway department's crew had evidently been caught in mid-repair by the outbreak of the war.

Rather than backtrack Hamlinward, Ellery had chanced a detour. He had long since regretted the gamble. The rutted and rotted dirt failed to connect with the

1

state highway. After hours of jouncing, Ellery was convinced that it was no detour at all but a lost wagon trail of the pioneers, leading nowhere.

He began to feel uneasy about water.

He saw no signs. He did not even know if he was still in California or had crossed into Nevada.

The sweet-burn odor died. He had forgotten it by the time he saw the wooden building up ahead.

Ellery should have set out for Hollywood earlier, but the prospect of bucking the pre-Christmas traffic and spending the holiday alone in a motor court somewhere had decided him to wait. That and the remark of the chain-smoking government man with whom he had discussed his trip. "The way things stand, Mr. Queen, we can spare gas for your car a lot easier than space on a plane or train. Or, for that matter, a bus."

In that December of 1943, depots and terminals and waiting rooms across the land demanded *Is This Trip Necessary?* and they were all packed with people who clearly thought the answer was yes. Businessmen waving priorities; students pointing home for their last civilian vacations; recruits on noisy boot leave; beribboned brass in perfect custom-made uniforms; combat veterans wrapped in silence; and, everywhere, sweethearts and pregnant brides and wives clutching children "going to see my daddy—he's a soldier," or sailor, or Marine, or airman, or Coast Guardsman—servicemen unable to wangle a Christmas furlough. And it was all strident with gaiety: "He'll be so happy. He's never seen the baby!" and tears: "Then I'll *stand*. I don't need a seat. Please?" and the unspoken, unspeakable words: *But I've got to get there, I may never see him again.*

"I'll drive," Ellery had said.

So he had spent Christmas Eve at home with his father and the radio. Christmas Day brought church, unrationed turkey, and a walk in Central Park. After which the Inspector snugged down with his latest leisure project, a rereading of Gibbon's *Decline and Fall*—replete with clucks over the misdeeds of some royal Byzantine gangster—while Ellery wrote appallingly overdue letters.

On the twenty-sixth he had packed and rested for the journey ahead, which he contemplated with no joy whatsoever. He had been working hard and his bones lacked bounce. At eight the next morning he piled his suitcases into the antique Duesenberg, embraced his father, and took off.

By some leer of fate, several of the servicemen he picked up early in the trip spelled him at the wheel while he was still fresh; but after he crossed the Mississippi, when he was beginning to feel the strain, not one of the hitchhikers he stopped for proved able to drive or had a license. So by the evening of December 31, when he pulled into a Hollywood already boiling over with New Year's Eve good cheer, he was weary in every cell and desperate for a hot bath and a good mattress.

"I know, Mr. Queen," said the desk clerk with the basset eyes, "I *know* we confirmed your reservation. But . . ." It seemed that Ellery's room had been boarded by two ensigns freshly in from the South Pacific.

"And in the finest tradition of the Navy," sighed Ellery, "they won't give up the ship. All right, I'm licked. Where's the nearest phone?" But by this time he had to find it for himself.

Lew Walsh exclaimed. "Ellery! You bet we can put you up. For as long as you like. Get over here pronto. The party's going good."

It certainly was. But he was unable to back out with grace, and it was almost dawn before he achieved the bath and the mattress. His sleep was turbulent. Voices howled faintly in his inner ear; he rocketed down an endless white line on an endless highway; and his fingers ached from steering with the sheet.

From time to time the world of his senses coupled with the world of his dreams and spawned phantasmagoria. Once he saw a splash of sunlight, smelled roses growing in freshly watered earth; but then his eyes slid shut again and he struggled into a dark dusk somewhere in the mountain snows, snows stained with splotches of blood like roses. Another time a radio voice pronounced a passionate *Helen!*, and immediately he was being tossed between the gong tormented sea of Homer and a modern ocean hellishly aglare with exploding ships, while gongs sounded and resounded and the tormented sea roared in agony.

He slept until dark, and he was still tired when he awoke, the hot shower barely lapping at the shores of his tiredness. Evelyn Walsh pounced on him—"We thought you'd died in your sleep, Ellery!"—and proceeded to stuff him with orange juice and eggs and toast and pancakes and brassy tea ("We're out of bacon and coffee, darn it." It seemed the Walshes had been prodigal with their ration stamps). Ellery sipped the tea thinly; he had envisioned coffee by the quart.

Lew Walsh gave him his choice between joining them in a quiet New Year's Night get-together at the home of a movie-star friend of theirs in the Hills or "just sitting around the house yakking." Having experienced quiet New Year's Night get-togethers in Hollywood, Ellery shamelessly chose the alternative. They talked the war, and the flesh situation—Lew was a partner in a. talent agency—and the Nazi concentration-camp stories, and the voices began to go away, and then Ellery heard Evelyn say, "That does it," and his head jerked up and his eyes flew open. "You're going right back to bed, Ellery Queen, if I have to undress you myself."

"Well . . . but will you and Lew go to your party?"

"Yes. Now *march*."

When he opened his eyes it was midway through Sunday afternoon. He was still wrung to the withers. And something new had been added, a case of the shakes.

"What's the *matter* with you?" his hostess asked. She had rustled a bit of coffee somewhere, and he was trying to hold the cup steady as he gulped. "You look awful."

"I can't seem to throw off this fatigue, Evelyn."

Lew Walsh shook his head. "If you feel this way now, Ellery, how are you going to live through the rat race? I understand this O.W.I. fellow you're to work for at Metropolitan is trying to win the war all by himself."

Ellery closed his eyes and said, "More coffee? Please?"

The next morning he made it a point to get to the Metropolitan lot at nine o'clock—by Hollywood writers' standards the middle of the night. He found Lieutenant-Colonel Donaldson waiting for him with a chill smile.

"Too much New Year's, Queen?" The chicken colonel's eyes were clear as a schoolboy's. "I'd better make it understood right off that the early bird isn't caught napping. I run a tight little cadre here. Know Charley Dyers?"

"Hi, Charley," said Ellery. If Charley Dyers was already at work by 9:00 A.M. on the Monday after the New Year's weekend, Colonel Donaldson ran a tight little cadre indeed. Dyers had been hacking out screenplays since the days when the close-up was a daring innovation.

"Hi, sonny," said the old-timer, and he squinted down his ruby nose to the inch-long ash on his cigar. "Welcome to the Espreeda Corps."

"Yes. Well," said Colonel Donaldson. "Queen, are you familiar with what we're doing here?"

"Somebody told me the other night that the screenplays deal with subjects like The Importance of Keeping Flies Out of Mess Halls and V.D. Will Get You If You Don't Watch Out."

The colonel's chill look formed ice. "He doesn't know what he's talking about. V.D.'s being handled by another unit altogether."

Ellery glanced at Charley Dyers, but Dyers was gazing innocently out the colonel's picture window, through which came the medicinal odor of peeling eucalyptus. Same old Hollywood. The only difference was the uniform on the man behind the De Mille-sized desk.

"All *right*," said Colonel Donaldson briskly. "We have three months—four at the outside—to prepare twenty screenplays, ten for service personnel, the rest for civilian viewing. Now, gentlemen, to quote a Chinese proverb, one picture is worth a thousand words, so you can figure out for yourselves how many words we've got to turn out to get these films in the can. And no time for mistakes," he added sternly. "To err is human, but in war you've got to be divine. Nobody's heard a shot fired in anger in this country since 1865, and most of us don't realize—simply do not realize—that we can lose this little old war." While Ellery was puzzling out this last juxtaposition of thoughts, the colonel pressed his attack with, "Well, the war's not going to be lost in *my* theater," in a voice of naked steel. "Teamwork, Queen! Remember that I represent the armed forces, Dyers the studio, and you . . ." For a moment the colonel seemed at a loss. "And you," he rallied, "you'll be working *with* us, Queen, not *for* us, and when I say work I mean . . . *work!*"

Work he did, belly to belly with a cursing Charley Dyers. Twelve hours a day, often longer. If Ellery had come to Hollywood worn out, he was soon in a state of ambulatory exhaustion.

Somehow the accommodations he had been promised by the Office of War Information melted away in a snafu and he found himself, feebly protesting, still in the tender billet of the Walshes. But Evelyn Walsh's mother-henning and Lew's unaggressive hospitality failed to make even the weekends tolerable. The colonel's Pavlovian discipline in early rising made it impossible for Ellery to sleep late on Sundays, so that on his day off he found himself going over, rather than getting over, the week's work—and cringing over the thought of Monday morning.

Even worse than Colonel Donaldson's hot spearmint-scented breath on his ear was the rewrite situation. No sooner had Ellery and Dyers settled down to a new script than back came the old one, or the old two or three or four, with demands for rewritten scenes, new scenes, cut scenes, bridges—revisions in wholesale lots. At least twice Ellery caught himself writing a scene into one script that belonged in another.

He and Dyers had long since stopped speaking to

each other except in command situations. Each labored
within a force-field of his own purgatory. With gray-dirt
faces and red-eyed as albinos they became prisoners of
the war, filled with eternal, hopeless hate.

The pay-off came on Saturday, the first of April. All
Fools' Day.

Ellery had checked into the studio that morning at
seven-thirty. How long he had been slogging away at the
typewriter he did not know; but suddenly he felt cold
hands on his, and he looked up to find Colonel Donaldson stooping over him.

"What?" Ellery said.

"I said what's the matter with you, Queen. Look!"

Ellery sighted along the colonel's military finger. It
was trained on the paper in the typewriter. *Richard
Queen Richard Queen Richard Queen,* he read. *Richard
Queen Richard . . .*

"I spoke to you," the colonel said. "You neither
looked at me nor answered. Just kept typing *Richard
Queen.* Who's Richard Queen? Your son?"

Ellery shook his head and immediately stopped. He
could have sworn something rattled inside, something
with a long extension, like a chain. "My father," he said,
and pushed cautiously away from the desk. When nothing happened, he gripped the edge and changed the
direction of the push from horizontal to vertical. This,
he found to his surprise, was considerably harder to do.
Also, his legs were quivering. Frowning, he clung to the
desk.

Colonel Donaldson was frowning, too. It was a chief-
of-staff-type frown, fraught with decisions for the further conduct of the war.

"Colonel," began Ellery, and stopped. Had he stuttered? It seemed to him he had stuttered. Or was hearing things. He inhaled smartly and tried again. "Colonel
. . ." There. That was perfect. And he was so very very
very very tired. "I think I've had it."

The colonel said, "I think you have." There was no
rancor in his voice. A cog in his military engine had
worn out; the sensible thing to do was replace it before

it snapped. Fortunes of war. "Glad it didn't happen sooner—we're almost to our objective. Well, well, we'll carry on. And oh," he said, "will you be all right, Queen?"

Will I be all right, thought Ellery. "No," he said. "Yes."

Colonel Donaldson nodded hastily and turned to go. But at the door he hesitated, as if he had just remembered something. "Well," he said, and cleared his throat. "Good show, Queen, good show!" And left.

Ellery sat wondering where Charley Dyers was. Probably out for a bourbon break. Good old Charley. The hell with him.

And New York. Oh, New York, its April damps and dirt-flecked beauty. California, here I go—back home and broken—with gratitude in my heart. To the comfortable, shabby old apartment. To the end of a Gotham day and the dearly beloved father-image in the threadbare bathrobe intent on leather-bound *Decline and Fall*. To rest. To rest. Did they give squeezed-out writers Purple Hearts?

And so it was that the next morning, before the Walshes were out of their circular bed—he had made his good-byes the night before—Ellery stowed his suitcases in the Duesenberg and drove out of Hollywood, eastward bound.

The wooden building, he realized later, came into sight almost a mile away, but he had not at first identified it as such. The air was clear enough; it was the undulating ground that now revealed, now concealed it. It might have been a set from a Western film except that it was not neat enough. "Ramshackle" had probably been the word for it from the beginning. There was no sign that it had ever known a coat of paint.

But a sign—a painted sign—there certainly was. It must have been five feet across. Its lettering, more ambitious than accomplished, read:

END-OF-THE-WORLD STORE

Otto Schmidt, *Prop.*

Last Chance To Buy Gas And

Supplies. Next Chance Is

Other Side of Desert

Ellery guessed that he might not be far from the southern edge of Death Valley; but in this country guesses were sibling to disaster, and he felt in no condition to face disaster. Also, the state of his fuel gauge made a stop for gas the better part of wisdom. And while the food hamper Evelyn Walsh had pressed on him was still untouched, who knew what lay ahead? Yes, it might be a smart idea to stop and see what he could pick up in the way of additional supplies—and, of course, information.

Ellery slanted the Duesenberg toward the rickety porch, wondering vaguely why he should feel it necessary to rationalize the stop. Perhaps it was because there was something about the place, a quality of unexpectedness. It stood quite alone in the sun-baked landscape. There was no other building, not even the ruin of one; no other car.

There was a wagon, however, hitched to two animals. At first he thought they were mules—smallish mules, to be sure, but their size was less matter for wonder than that they were there at all. He had never seen mules farther west than Texas. But then, as he turned off his ignition, he saw that they were not mules; they were donkeys. Not the stunted burros of Old Prospector fame, but a more robust variety, like the asses of the Near East—handsome beasts, well-bred and well-fed.

Ellery had never seen their like outside films and paintings, and it was only the exhaustion which rode him like the Burr-Woman of the Indians that kept him from going over for a closer look. Supplies lay heaped beside the wagon: sacks, crates, cartons.

But then he forgot the wagon and the beasts. For in the silence left by the cutting off of his motor he heard men's voices, slow and deep. They were coming from inside the store. He backed heavily out of the Duesenberg and moved toward the porch as if he were wading through swells.

The boards of the porch wavered under his feet, and he walked even more gingerly. At the screen door he paused to rest. Then, as he was about to open it, the door opened seemingly by itself. Ellery was pondering this phenomenon when two men stepped through the doorway, two very strange and strangely dressed men.

It was the eyes of the first man, by far the elder of the two, that seized him. Later he was to think: *He has the eyes of a prophet;* but that was not his thought at the time. What came into his head at the moment of meeting were words from the Song of Songs: *Thine eyes are dove's eyes;* and with this, instantly, the knowledge that they were not dove's eyes at all. The eyes of an eagle? But no, there was nothing fierce or predatory about them. They were black-bright, blazing black-bright, like twin suns viewed with the naked eye. And there was something far-seeing about them. And yet non-seeing, too. It was the queerest thing. Perhaps—that was it!— they saw something that was there for only them to see.

He was tall, this strange man; bone-thin tall, and exceedingly old. In his eighties, certainly; possibly his nineties. His skin had been so worked upon by time and the sun that it was weathered almost black. From his chin fell a small sparse beard of yellowed white hair; his face otherwise was quite hairless. He was clothed in a robe, a robe with the cut and flow of an Arabian burnoose or *jallābiyah,* made of some unsophisticated cloth whose bleach had come, not from processed chemicals, but directly from the sun. He wore sandals on bare feet; he carried a staff taller than himself. And on his shoulder he bore a keg of nails with no sign of strain.

No actor could play this man, Ellery swiftly thought (the denial reaching his mind's surface even faster than the thought it denied—that the old man was here from

Hollywood, on location for some Biblical production). He was not made up for a part; he was really aged; in any case he would be inimitable. This old man could only *be,* Ellery thought. He *is.* An original.

The old man moved by him. The extraordinary eyes had rested a moment on his face and then had gone on —not so much past him as through him.

The second man was commonplace only by contrast with the old man. He, too, was sun-black—if a shade less darkened than the ancient, perhaps only because he was half the ancient's age. In his early forties, Ellery guessed; his beard was glossy black. The younger man's garments were made from the same odd cloth, but they were of an entirely different character—a simple blouselike shirt, without a collar and open at the throat; and trousers that reached only far enough down to cover his calves. He carried a hundred-pound sack on each shoulder, one of salt, the other of sugar.

The eyes of this younger man were a clear-water gray, and they rested briefly on Ellery's face with shy curiosity. The gray eyes shifted to look over at the Duesenberg, and they widened with an awe rarely inspired by that venerable vehicle except on the score of its age. The glance returned to Ellery for another shy moment; then the younger man moved after the elder and went over to the wagon and began to load the supplies.

Ellery stepped into the store. After the inferno outside, its dim coolness received him like a Good Samaritan; for a moment he simply stood there accepting its ministrations and looking about. It was a poor store, with sagging shelves scantily stocked and a dusty foliage of assorted articles hanging from the tin ceiling. The store proper was far too shallow to comprise the entire building, Ellery saw; there was a door at the rear, almost blocked by a stack of cardboard cartons imprinted *Tomatoes,* that probably led to a storeroom.

Along one side of the store ran a flaked and whittled counter; behind the counter, over a lop-eared ledger, stooped a roly-poly little man with a patch of seal mustache in the middle of his round and ruddy face—ob-

viously the Otto Schmidt, *Prop.*, of the sign. He did not
look up from his ledger.

So Ellery stood there, not so much observing as ab-
sorbing, taking a sensual pleasure in the laving coolness;
and then the tall old man came back into the store,
moving very quietly. He went over to the counter, his
blackened hand slipping into a slit in the side of his garment; it came out with something, and this something he
laid on the counter before the roly-poly proprietor.

Schmidt looked up. In that instant he spotted Ellery.
He snatched the something and pocketed it. But not before Ellery saw what it was.

It was a coin, large enough to be a silver dollar, and
remarkably bright and shiny, almost as if it were new.
But no new silver dollars had been minted for years.
Perhaps, he thought dully, perhaps it was a foreign coin.
There were colonies of bearded sectarians, Old Russian
in origin, in Mexico . . .

But dollar, or peso—whatever the coin was—the
heap of supplies being loaded onto the wagon seemed
far too much to be paid for by a single piece of silver.

Neither the old man nor the man behind the counter
uttered a word. Evidently all arrangements had been
made before Ellery came in, leaving no need for further
conversation. Once more the glance shafted through
him; then, incredibly erect, incredibly light on his san-
daled feet, the old man left the store. The mystery was
not to be resisted; and even if the will to resist had been
there, Ellery was too exhausted to exercise it. He followed.

In time to see the old man set one foot on the wagon
wheel and lift himself easily to the high seat, where the
younger man was now perched. And to hear him speak
for the second time, for one of the slow, deep voices Ellery had heard on first approaching the store had been
this voice.

"Very well, Storicai."

Storicai? At least that was how it sounded. Storicai
. . . What a queer name! Ellery could not fix it in point
of time or place. And oh, that voice, the voice that had

uttered it, so rich with power, so tranquil—a voice with the strangest accent, and infinitely at peace . . .

Ellery sighed and shook his head as he went back into the store. Distracted now only by the memory and not the presence, he allowed the store to sink into his pores: its musty fragrance of old wood, coffee beans, kerosene, spices, tobacco, vinegar, and coolness—above all, coolness.

"Never saw anything like that before, did you?" the storekeeper said cheerfully; and Ellery agreed that no, he never had. "Well," the storekeeper went on, "it's a free country, and they don't bother nobody. What can I do for you?"

He could fill the Duesenberg up with high-test was what he could do. No high-test? No call for it on a back road like this. Well, all right, regular would do. It would have to. What? Oh, yes, he had stamps for the gas . . . Otto Schmidt came back and took Ellery's ten-dollar bill as if he had never seen one before, and rumpled his cowlick once or twice, and made change. Anything else?

Ellery glanced about, thinking there was something more he wanted; he ordered tobacco for his pipe, paid for it, looked around again . . . there was still something . . .

"How about some supper?" suggested Mr. Schmidt shrewdly. And all at once Ellery realized that this was exactly what he wanted. He nodded.

"Just take a seat at the table there. Ham and eggs, coffee and pie be all right? I could open a can of soup—"

"Ham and eggs, coffee and pie will do just fine." He felt guilty about Evelyn's still unopened box lunch, but it was hot food he wanted. He sat down at the table. It was bare of cloth but quite clean; and there was a much-handled copy of the *Reese River Reveille and Austin Sun* dated the previous November.

Austin . . . that was in Nevada—it couldn't be Texas. Or California. So he must be in Nevada. Or—no, that didn't follow. Anyone coming west from Nevada could have left it just about here. He would ask Mr.

Schmidt what state they were in. But Mr. Schmidt was frying ham in the kitchen; and by the time he returned, the question had left Ellery's mind.

Ham and eggs, coffee and pie appeared on the table simultaneously. All were surprisingly good for a country store in the middle of nowhere. Even the pie had a surprise to it. In addition to a crisp, brown, flaky crust, the fruit was just the right mixture of tart and sweet, with a spicy flavor that reminded Ellery of cinnamon; but there was something else, too.

He looked up and saw that Mr. Schmidt was smiling. "It's clove," said Mr. Schmidt.

"Yes," Ellery agreed. "I did smell the clove, but I thought it was from the ham. Delicious."

The proprietor's moon face was split by a grin. "Where I come from there are a lot of Cornishmen— Cousin Jacks, we called them—and they used to put clove in their pie instead of cinnamon. I thought to myself, Why not both?—and I've been putting in both ever since."

Ellery indicated the chair opposite him. "How about joining me in a cup of coffee?"

"Well, say. Thank you!" beamed Otto Schmidt; and he brought a cup of coffee from the kitchen and sat down and began to talk as if Ellery had opened a stopvalve. His delight in company and conversation was that of a man who did not often get much of either.

He was from Wisconsin originally, it seemed—a small city in the northern part of the state—where he had run his father's neighborhood grocery store.

"Just about gave me a living," Schmidt said. "After Pop died I had no family in the United States, so I was kind of lonesome as well as scraping along. Then two bad things happened more or less together . . ."

The depression had settled on the land, and Schmidt's health had broken down. His doctor had advised a warm, dry climate; the growing inability of his customers to pay their grocery bills had put an end to the matter.

"The store had been owned by my family for over

forty years," the stout little man said, "but I had no choice. Paid my suppliers, marked down everything, cleared off the shelves, and found myself heading west with five hundred dollars in my pockets and not an idea in the world where I was going or what I was going to do. Then my jalopy ran out of gas about a mile from here. I hiked in and found a fellow named Parslow running this store. He was fed up with it and I offered him the five hundred for the place, lock, stock, and barrel, half in cash. He held out for three hundred down. 'Tell you what I'll do,' I told him. 'My car's a mile up the road and it doesn't need a thing but gas. You can have her for the other fifty.' 'Done!' he says. We closed the deal and he filled up a can with gasoline and was all set to start walking. 'Haven't you forgotten something?' I ask. 'What?' he says, patting his pockets. 'That'll be fifty cents for the gasoline,' I says. Well, he swore at me, but he paid. And that was how I came to be here, and I've been here ever since."

And he chuckled with satisfaction. He would never go back, he assured Ellery. He made very little money, but even on his once-a-year trips to Los Angeles he was always glad to get back. It was . . . He hesitated, his pudgy hands making exploratory circles in the air. It was so *clean* out here on the edge of the desert. You could see for miles in the daytime, and at night . . . oh, you could see for *millions* of miles.

"How about those two fellows who were here when I arrived?" Ellery asked suddenly. "Who are they?"

"Oh, they live out in the desert somewhere. Hermits."

"Hermits?"

"Sort of. Don't know what they do for grub generally —they come to the store here only a couple times a year. Nice folks, though. Queer, maybe, but like I said, they don't bother nobody. Everybody's got a right to go his own way, so long as he don't bother nobody, is what I always say."

Ellery remarked that he couldn't agree more, and rose. Mr. Schmidt swiftly suggested more pie and coffee in a transparent maneuver to detain him. Ellery smiled faintly, shook his head, settled his bill, and then said that he had better get some directions before going on.

"Directions for where?" the little man asked. Ellery looked pained. Where indeed?

"Las Vegas," he said.

Schmidt took Ellery by the arm and marched him to the door. Here, with many gestures, corrections, and repetitions, he described a route. Boiled down—as nearly as Ellery could remember afterward—it came to this: "Follow this road along the edge of the desert. Don't take any of the roads that go off to the left. When you come to the first fork, bear right. That's the road that leads you onto the main highway for Las Vegas."

Ellery waved good-bye and drove off. He expected never to see the End-of-the-World Store or Otto Schmidt, *Prop.*, again.

Once again he drove off toward home, reversing the path of the pioneers—for that matter, of the sun itself. The hot meal had added its own inducement toward drowsiness to his exhaustion, and he had to fight a running battle with it.

He kept his eyes open for the "first fork" in the road, where he was to bear right for the highway that led to Las Vegas. Once—perhaps twice, he was not sure—he noticed a wide path (it seemed little more) which he took to be one of the roads that "go off to the left," and he avoided it with a minor sense of triumph. He had forgotten to ask Otto Schmidt how far away Las Vegas was and how long he might have to be on the road.

The day was settling into its decline, and he began to entertain an only half-amusing fantasy that he was not going to reach any recognizable destination that night. It made him think of the legend of Peter Rugg. The Missing Man, New England's version of The Flying Dutchman, who defied the heavenly elements and for punishment was condemned to gallop in his phantom chaise forever with a thunderstorm at his back, trying to reach a Boston that forever eluded him. Perhaps, Ellery thought, future travelers would repeat the tale of the ancient Duesenberg and its phantom driver, eternally stopping to inquire if he was on the right road to Las Vegas!

Try as he would to keep not only his sleepy eyes but his drifting mind on the road (". . . *first fork . . . turn right . . .*"), Ellery's thoughts kept circling back to the old man with the curious speech, the curious costume, the curiously powerful serenity. Funny old bird to meet in the year 1944, of the independence of the United States the 168th, even in a timeless desert. Was there ever an age when that old man would not have commanded attention, a fascination not far removed from awe?

A clump of desert willows pink with blossoms caught his eye; in the next moment he had forgotten them, but perhaps they sparked his mental leap backward over whole millennia to another time and desert and *jallābiyah*-clad people among whom moved men like that old man—men called patriarchs, or prophets, or apostles.

That old man of the wagon and his *"Very well, Storicai,"* in an English flavored with that strange accent—no, not of those Russian sectarians in Mexico after all . . . It was not his accent, or his voice, or his face, or his garb that was so remarkable, although together they were remarkable enough. Rather it was his ineffable composure, a certain extraordinary aura of . . . grandeur? No, no! What was the word?

Righteousness, that was it. Not self righteousness, but righteousness . . . unswerving rectitude . . . acceptance with God . . . It blazed from his eyes. That was it! How very, very remarkable were the eyes of that old man . . .

Much later, recalling the dreamlike journey, Ellery came to believe that in his half-hallucinated state, while reflecting on the eyes of the old man, his own eyes had failed to see the fork in the road of which Otto Schmidt had spoken. Certainly he had not borne right, as Schmidt had instructed him. He must have borne left instead.

He was to remember how, floating between reflection and exhaustion, he realized that the road he was traveling had definitely stopped skirting the desert and had crept into it. Joshua trees thrust their spiky limbs every which way, as if groping blindly for something; the frail scent of sand verbena kept touching his nostrils . . .

. . . until it was replaced gently and slowly and, thus, imperceptibly, until all at once the verbena scent was gone, blocked out by something stronger, heavier, more recently familiar . . .

. . . the smoke of sagebrush burning.

Again.

He frowned, blinked, noticed—consciously for the first time—how the road had changed. The graded dirt had given way to ungraded dirt, then to sand. Before he could think this out, he noticed that it was little more than a weedy trail embraced by two narrow ruts. He did not even then think: I am on the wrong road, and I had better turn around now while there is still enough light. He thought: It must be a very old automobile that uses this road, perhaps a Model T . . . And then: No, no automobile uses this road, because there is not a trace of oil on the weeds running down the middle of it.

With that, Ellery stopped the car and looked around. There was nothing but desert on all sides—creosote bushes, the grayish humps of burro-weed, the thorny crowns of yuccas, rocks, boulders, sand. He had stopped the car providentially. The road came to an end just ahead of him, on a rise. What was on the other side he preferred not to dwell on. Perhaps a sheer drop—a cliff.

The light was beginning to pale, and Ellery hastily stood up in the car and craned.

He saw at once that the rise was part of the rim of a low circular hill—a hill with a valley inside; or so it seemed in the failing light. A valley like the bottom of a shallow bowl, hence not really a valley at all, but a basin. Geological niceties, however, were far from his thoughts. As *valley* it first came into his tired mind; as *valley* it was to remain there.

While he stood in the rising heat of the motor, gazing at the rim of hill, a figure suddenly rose from the crest to become fixed in silhouette between the lemon-yellow sky and the hill beyond, already deepening from pink to

rose-red . . . while he watched, to purple. Hooded robe
from which emerged gaunt profile and jutting beard,
long staff in one hand, and in the other . . . It was, it had
to be, it could be no other than the old man of the wagon
at the End-of-the-World Store.

For a timeless interval Ellery stood there, in the Duesenberg, half convinced that he was the victim of a desert
mirage, or that the appearance of this archetype of all
father-figures was related in some way to his recent
withdrawal from awareness of the world, characterized
by the senseless repetition of his father's name on the
studio typewriter . . . He saw the curiously thin-look-
ing figure on the hill—as sharp against the sky as if
there were no thickness to him at all—raise something
to his lips.

A trumpet?

In the silence (literally breathless for him, for he was
holding his breath) Ellery heard, or fancied he heard,
an unearthly sound. It was at once alien yet hauntingly
familiar. Not the long, archaic silvern trumpets that had
heralded the proclamation of the British king (and,
eight months later, of his brother); not the harsh, yet
tremendously stirring ram's horn, the shofar of the synagogue, confuting Satan as it jarred slumbering sinners
to repentance; nor the baroque *boo-boo*ing of the conch
shell whereby the hundred thousand avatars of Brahma
are summoned to compassion; not the horns of Elfland,
faintly blowing; nor the sweet-cracked melancholy jazz
of the cornet at an old-time New Orleans funeral . . .
it was like none of these, yet it evoked something of all
these . . .

If, indeed, he had heard anything. At all.

As in a dream, Ellery turned off the ignition and got
out of his car and walked in the direction of the silhouette, the long strange echo of the trumpet still in his
ears. (Or was it only the singing silence of the sands?)

He began to climb the low hill.

And as he climbed, the tall figure achieved a third di-
mension and turned toward him. The hand that did not
grasp the staff was not visible now; it was buried in the

folds of the robe . . . holding the trumpet? Ellery could not tell. What he could tell, however, and surely, was that this was indeed the old man of the wagon. And as Ellery reached the summit, the old man began to speak.

He spoke in English, as before, the same curiously accented English that struck the ear with such unfamiliarity. Or it might be not so much an accent as an intonation. What was the old man saying? Ellery frowned, concentrating.

"The Word be with you."

That must have been what he said. And yet . . . Perhaps it had not been *word* at all, but *ward*. Or *Lord*. There had been a distinct cadenced hesitation in the pronunciation, almost as if it were *Wor'd*. Or—

"World?" Ellery thought aloud.

The old man looked at him with a kindling eye. "Who are you?" he asked Ellery.

And again uncertainty followed. Surely there was a glottal stop after the *r* in *are,* the way the old man pronounced it? Or had he actually asked, *Who art thou?*—speaking the *thou* after the fashion of the British Quakers, so that it sounded more like *thu?*

In these uncertainties Ellery was certain of only one thing—that he felt queerly light-headed. Had he gained enough altitude since leaving the store so that a thinning atmosphere was affecting him? Or was it the exertion of the climb up the hill in his ever-mounting fatigue? He planted his feet apart for better support (how silly if he should faint now!) and he was aware with annoyance how slurred the words sounded as he said, "My name is Ellery—"

Before he could finish, an astounding thing happened. The old man bent double and began to fall. Instinctively Ellery reached out both hands to catch him, thinking that he was fainting, or even dying. But the old man slipped through his hands and landed on both knees on the sand, and he plucked the dusty cuff of Ellery's trouser, and he kissed it.

And while Ellery stared down open-mouthed, convinced that he was in the presence of senility, or madness, the old man prostrated himself; and he said something; and he said it again as he raised his head.

"Elrocc."

That was how his name sounded in the old man's curious accent. And Ellery felt his flesh ripple and chill. For wasn't there mention somewhere in the Bible of *Elroï,* or *Elroy?* Which meant . . . *God Sees?* Or *God Sees Me? . . .*

All this happened in seconds—his pronouncement of his Christian name, the old man's instant genuflection and repetition of the name in his own version—so that automatically Ellery went on to add his surname.

"—Queen."

And once more the astounding thing happened. For at the sound of *Queen* the old man again kissed the cuff of Ellery's trouser (*the hem of my garments!* Ellery thought, half angrily), again prostrated himself in the dust; and again he repeated what Ellery had said, again giving it a curious and unfamiliar quality.

"Quenan," the old man was saying. "Quenan . . . Quenan . . ."

But this version of his surname brought no shock of recognition. *Quenan . . . ?*

And the old man, still on his knees, went on and on; but what he was saying was meaningless to Ellery, whose own train of thought wandered afield. The hand he had reflexively extended to catch the old man, he was amazed to find, was resting on the old man's cowled head. How had it got there? Surely by accident. Good Lord! he thought. The old boy will think I'm blessing him. And he stifled an impulse to grin. He could make out nothing of what the bearded patriarch was saying— a swift mutter of unrecognizable words that might even have been a prayer.

Ellery came to himself. The old man had risen and taken Ellery's hand in his; and in his odd eyes there was something like excitement (though not exactly that) and something less than concern (though almost that). And he said to Ellery, quite intelligibly, "The time of plowing is over, the days of waiting are at an end."

Ellery searched his memory. Was the old hermit quoting something? No, nothing Ellery could recognize. And where was the younger hermit?

"The time of the threshing of the harvest is here, and the great trouble is soon to come upon us."

"No, Ellery decided, nothing he was familiar with.

"Art thou the first?"

The question rang in Ellery's ears.

"The first?" he repeated foolishly.

"The first. He who comes to us in the time of our great trouble, and prepares the way for the second. Praised be the Wor'd."

No doubt about it now—some sort of slight pause in *Wor'd*. But what could it all mean? He could only look into those unfathomable eyes and repeat, "The second?"

The old man nodded slowly. "The second shall be first, and the first shall be second. It is written thus. We thank thee, O Wor'd."

Had the statement been uttered by another man, Ellery might have passed it off as gibberish, a paraphrase of some imagined Scripture. But this man—"the old, old, very old man"—this man compelled respect. Almost he compelled belief.

"Who are you?" Ellery asked.

"Truly thou knowest me," the prophetic mouth smiled gravely. "I am the Teacher."

"And the name of this place?"

A silence, briefly. Then, "I had forgotten that you are a stranger here, even though your coming is a sign that the Wor'd is sure to follow. The place where we stand goes by the name of Crucible Hill, and below us is the Valley of Quenan. This name you know, seeing that it is your own. And what you are cannot be hidden from you." He bowed.

My God, Ellery thought, he's mistaken me for someone else, someone he's been waiting for. A tragicomedy of coincidence, based on nothing more substantial than a similarity of sounds. But whom has he mistaken me for? On hearing my name, Ellery, he prostrated himself in humblest reverence, thinking I had said *"Elroï,"* or *"Elroy"*—*"thou, God, seest me."* He took me for . . .

Ellery could not bring himself to believe it.

Through the giddiness he fought against, he heard the old man—"the Teacher"—saying, "My people do not know the mystery that is to be; they do not know the trouble which is coming upon them, nor how to save themselves when the hailstorm dashes the crop to the earth. They have lived as children. What will they do when the fire rages?"

His grip on Ellery's hand tightened. "Come," he said, "come and abide with us."

Ellery heard his voice asking from far away, "For how long?"

And said the old man, "Until thy work is done."

Tucking his staff under his arm, the other hand still hidden by his robe (holding the trumpet?—had there been a trumpet?), he gently drew Ellery forward and began to walk him down the inner slope of the hill.

And Ellery stepped into another world. It was so startling that almost he cried out. One moment he had been in a desert of sand and naked rock, the next he was descending into a land green and fat with trees and grass and growing crops. In the basin formed by the circle of hills the soil had been terraced; plow ridges ran along the natural contours of the land. In the twilight's hush he heard the pleasant sound of water trickling, and when he turned in the direction of the sound he saw a rivulet emerging from underground and obediently following the course laid out for it. Plainly some master hand had directed with love and skill this conversion of the desert, so that no grain of earth, no drop of water, should go to waste.

And now, far down the slope, he noticed for the first time a settlement. There were enough houses to constitute a village—fifty of them, he estimated, most of them small, a very few larger, and all of the simplest construction. And then an evening breeze came up, and he heard faint voices; and the breeze brought with it a scent of smoke, which he could see rising in slow spirals from the houses.

It was the odor of burning sagebrush.

They were halfway down the slope when the sun set abruptly behind the western shoulder of the hill.

A great shadow fell quickly over the valley of—what had the old man called it?—Quenan.

Ellery shivered.

II

MONDAY

April 3.

THE EYE HAD been looking at Ellery unblinking for a long time before he could bring himself to consider it. His attention once directed at it, it ceased to be an eye and became—obviously—a knothole.

Aye, tear her tattered ensign down—

"That's enough of that nonsense!" he said firmly, sitting up. His sudden movement sent the worn clean quilt sliding to the floor—a journey of no great distance, he learned immediately, since he had been sleeping on sheepskins spread over a tick stuffed with hay and corn shucks. The smell of all three was plain. He was not in some primitive motor court after all.

And with that, he remembered.

As had happened before and was to happen again, he got up believing he was fully rested; the ache in his bones he attributed to his having slept without a mattress or bedsprings.

He automatically looked around for a shower but there was none; he saw no sign of plumbing. The crude cottage had three small rooms, sparingly equipped with furniture as primitive and unpainted as the cottage itself. But all the wood glowed with a patina that gave off a definite odor. Ellery sniffed at a chair. Beeswax . . .

On one of the tables lay a lump of homemade soap, a length of clean cloth evidently intended as a towel, and a salt-glazed water pitcher and bowl and cup. The pitcher was full. His luggage was neatly stacked in a corner of the room.

He took a sponge bath, gasping, then got into clean clothes. He brushed his teeth, combed his hair. Shaving . . . no hot water . . .

From the door came the rap of wood on wood. "Come in," Ellery said. He braced himself.

The Teacher entered. In one hand was his staff, in the other a basket. "Bless the Wor'd for the blessing of your coming," the old man said sonorously; and then he smiled. Ellery's answering smile was partly directed to himself for indulging a conceit: what could the old man's burden be but the fairy-tale basket of goodies? To his astonishment, that was what it proved to be—napkin covering and all.

"Commonly I dine alone," the Teacher said. "And it may be that you will sometimes wish to eat with the community in the dining hall. This first meal, however, I wish us to share, and here."

There was a fruit juice strange to Ellery (later he learned that it was a blend of mulberry and cactus pear); its flavor was bland and respectful of a nervous morning stomach. There was a platter of cornmeal pancakes with butter and syrup—probably sorghum or sorgo. Ellery missed his coffee, but the milk (it was ewe's milk, very rich) was warming and the gourd of herb tea, hot and sweetened with honey, made an interesting substitute.

Except for the old man's whispered prayers as he washed his hands and ate and drank, the meal proceeded in silence.

"Are you content with this food?" the Teacher asked at last.

"Yes," said Ellery. "I am content."

"Blessed be the Wor'd, and we are thankful . . . We may now go." He brushed the table clean of crumbs, repacked the basket, and rose.

Puddles of sunlight lay along the tree-lined lane which they followed to a building of gray stone. A murmur of childish voices became audible as they approached. Small rooms, each containing a table and two benches, opened off the main hall where the children were assembled. Of course, Ellery thought, without surprise: he is the Teacher—this must be the school.

The smallest children sat up front on the lowest benches; girls sat on one side, boys on the other. They rose as the Teacher confronted them. Row on row of shyly smiling, grave, or respectfully curious faces—all sun-tanned, all clean, all devoid of apathy or insolence —row on row to the teen-agers at the rear. Ellery saw each face clearly, and each face was clear.

"My children," said the Teacher. "Let us bless the Wor'd."

No head was bowed, no eye closed, no word spoken. An intense silence settled over the room. Dust motes, dancing in the sunbeams from the unglazed windows, seemed to move more slowly. A bird lifted up its song not far off.

"This is a great thing," the Teacher said. "You have all been guests in one another's houses. Now there is a guest among us who is a guest of all, of all Quenan. His coming is a gift to us of the greatest importance. I will tell you now only that it has been foretold. What he is to do, you will all witness. To the Wor'd, our thanks for sending him. This is today's lesson. We shall keep today as a holiday. You may go home now; you may put on your holiday robes, you may play or study or help your parents as you wish. Now, go. Blessed is the Wor'd."

He passed among them, touching the head of one, the shoulder of another, lightly patting a cheek or an arm. The children looked wonderingly at Ellery, but they did not speak to him. The boys were dressed in the fashion of Storicai, the old man's companion at the End-of-the-World Store—collarless shirt and "clam-digger" pants; the girls wore long one-piece dresses. All were barefoot. Presently he was to see them emerge from their houses like figures in a Biblical painting, yet with no hint of masquerade; some carried flowers.

Ellery walked with his guide through the village, accepting with wonder the occasional flower offered to him, even by the older boys.

"Do you have many visitors—guests—from outside?" Ellery asked. And found himself adding, "Teacher?"

"None," said the Teacher.

"None? In the past, surely—?"

"In the past, none. You are the first—as it is written. We know little of the outside, and the outside knows nothing of us."

The light shineth in the darkness, and the darkness comprehendeth it not.

Ellery observed the village with mounting excitement.

Nestled in their patches of garden, the weathered little cottages were bare of ornamentation except for vines, which had been allowed to overrun the walls. The natural wood had turned silvery gray and yellow-brown, with an occasional splash of ochre; the green of the vines and plants and the multicolors of the flowers completed a chromatic harmony that brought peace to the eye. And for contrast there was the rough and random stone of the few larger, public buildings.

Visually the dwellings had a curious vitality, as if they too had grown out of the earth. And here was a lesson, Ellery thought, for architects. It was as if art (or artfulness) was not so much frowned on here as unheard of. There was an artless beauty about it, an innocence, a natural functionalism that, when he thought of the mathematical *Bauhaus*-style urban boxes or Le Corbusier's machines for living, made him wince.

There was no paving. There was no electricity. There were no telephone lines. Barns and farmland and pasture revealed no combustion-engine equipment; even the plows were mostly of wood. And yet everything was lush and teeming. It was hard to remember that beyond the circle of the hills—Crucible Hill, had the old man said?—lay all but lifeless desert.

And the people . . .

Now and then a woman came out on her doorstep to greet the Teacher respectfully, a respect tinged with something remotely like uneasiness, as if the newness and wonder of the guest had suddenly overshadowed everything. Or a man on his way to the fields, or returning —feet stained with earth, hoe on shoulder, gourd of water in hand—would greet the Teacher; and again the eyes would dart to the newcomer, and away, and back again.

Except for the children, free on their holiday, everyone was busied with some task; yet there was no air of drudgery, none of the tension or depression so often produced by industrial work. Everyone Ellery saw seemed happy and at peace.

In spite of an occasional browsing animal, the unpaved streets were remarkably clean, a phenomenon presently explained when they came upon the village's department of sanitation. It consisted of one very old man and one very young woman, who were raking the dirt of the lanes with whisklike implements and carefully depositing each twig and turd and leaf in a donkey cart.

The wonder in their eyes as they glanced at Ellery, and then hastily away, was as deep in the very old man as in the very young woman.

It was a wonder not confined to the people of Quenan. Ellery himself was filled with it. Here, indeed, was the Peaceable Kingdom.

Or so it seemed.

"Here we must stop awhile," said the Teacher, pausing before a large building, barn-size and barn-simple. The heat of the day had increased, and it was a relief to rest. This building had fewer windows than the school, and it was cool inside. Blinking in the dimness after the dazzling sun, Ellery located a bench and sat down.

They were evidently in a sort of central warehouse or supply depot. Shelves ranged the walls and divided the interior into sections; there were bins and compartments and drawers. Bunches of herbs hung drying and dried, wreaths of chili peppers, ropes of red onions glowing like embers in the half-light; white corn, and yellow corn, and Indian corn with kernels of every color from black to lavender; sacks of meal, dried beans in greater variety than Ellery had ever seen outside a Mexican or Puerto Rican grocery. He saw wheels of cheeses, bales of wool, dirt-brown on the outside and creamy white on the shorn underside; hanks of yarn, huge spools of thread, bolts of cloth, tools, parts of looms and spinning wheels, bundles of wax candles hanging by looped wicks, kegs of nails, packets of bone needles, heaps of horn combs, buttons, wooden spools, earthernware, seeds, even crocks of preserves.

It was a primitive cornucopia, a rude horn of plenty; and there was a counter of sorts behind which stood the man Storicai, who had been with the Teacher at Otto Schmidt's store. He greeted Ellery solemnly, his glance slipping past as if to see whether the guest had not, perhaps, come to the storehouse in that strange vehicle which had so fascinated him outside Schmidt's that day . . .

That day? It seemed like only yesterday—

Suddenly Ellery realized that it had been only yesterday.

The shock jolted him out of the sense of dream-participation which he had been experiencing. It was as if he had been caught in a time maze, in which past and present kept shifting like the colors of a kaleidoscope. Certain now, as he had not been a moment before, which day of the week it was (althouth he was by no means certain of the year, or, for that matter, of the century), Ellery watched the Teacher take a knife from some pocket or pouch within his robes and sliding it from its sheath show Storicai that the blade was broken.

"Shall I fetch you a new one, then?" asked the younger man.

"No—" the Teacher said. (Or was it "Nay"? What *was* that odd accent, or inflection? Had it developed from some originally minor quirk of speech by the Quenan community's isolation?—or from some other tongue?—or from both?) "—no, I shall choose one for myself. Each hand knows its own need best, Storesman. Place the broken one in the repairs bin for the Carpentersmith."

Murmuring, "So, Teacher," Storicai the Storesman obeyed (in a community like this, Ellery thought, waste-not-want-not would be more a matter of survival than of thrift); but the Storesman did so with his eyes still on the stranger, on and away and on and away.

The Teacher's voice came from the shadows. "When last you saw our guest, Storicai, you did not know, nor did I know, that he was to be here amongst us. He it is who was foretold. It is a great thing that has been visited upon us, Storesman, a very great thing." The voice, so old, so strong, fell silent.

The Storesman's eyes widened with that same wonder Ellery had seen throughout Quenan. Rather restlessly, Ellery stirred. A stray sunbeam picked out his wrist watch, and it glittered. The Storesman uttered a little cry.

"Oh," he said. "Oh."

"My wrist watch—"

"Oh!"

The watch was of gold, and wafer-thin, his father's birthday present to him of some years earlier. It showed not only the time of day but the day of the month as well, and the year, and the phases of the moon. Only the last, Ellery now thought, seemed fitting to this valley. New moon and old moon: what other reckoning was needed in this little lost land—land which time forgot, to its contentment?

"Haven't you ever seen a wrist watch?" Ellery asked, raising his arm.

The Storesman's bearded face was broad with amazement. "A timepiece to wear on the hand? No, no."

"Then you have seen watches of other kinds? And clocks?"

Ellery hoped that he did not sound like the mighty white man patronizing the child of nature. But it turned out that Storicai was familiar with watches and clocks. There were a few watches in Quenan (Ellery saw some

of them later—great, grave grandfathers of pocket time-
pieces, wound by key, which must have crossed the prai-
ries behind oxen leaning heavily into the endlessly
stretching grass), and a few clocks, too. "Clocks with
hands," the Storesman explained with pride, although it
appeared that most of them were hourglasses, and some
sundials ("for shadow-time") and some water clocks
("for night-time").

On impulse Ellery slipped the watch off his wrist.
Storicai's eyes opened even wider at the flexible action
of the metal-mesh band. "This is what it does," Ellery
said. "And this . . . and this."

"But the key. I see no keyhole."

"It keeps winding itself up, Storicai. Through the ordinary movements of the arm."

The Storesman touched the wrist watch timidly.
Again it glittered, and the glitter reflected from his eyes.
For a moment Ellery wondered if the gleam signified
wonder so much as cupidity. Or perhaps neither, he
thought. Or something else, or nothing else.

"Here is the new knife I have chosen," said the
Teacher, returning. "It fits my hand well."

The Storesman nodded, turning reluctantly from Ellery's watch. He drew toward him a huge ledgerlike
tome, a sort of log or daybook that looked homemade;
and in this tome he recorded the transaction of the
knives. When he was finished, Ellery—again on impulse
—held the wrist watch out to him. "I have another one I
can use while I am here," he said to Storicai. "Would
you like to wear this one until I leave?"

Storicai's eyes shone as he turned automatically to the
Teacher. And the old man smiled and nodded as if to a
child. Ellery slipped his watch over Storicai's thick wrist;
and as he and the Teacher left the storehouse. Ellery
glanced back to see the bearded man turning the gold
watch this way and that in the shaft of sunlight.

"Your temple, is that it?—or your, well, town hall?"
Ellery asked as they went into the tallest and most im-
posing of the stone public buildings. Each window was

set in a vertical recess almost the height of the structure.

"The Holy Congregation House," the Teacher said. "Here I have my room, and the Successor has his. Here is where the Crownsil meets, and here——"

"The what meets?" Ellery thought the old man's speech idiosyncrasy had corrupted the word "council."

But the old man repeated patiently, "Crownsil. In this hall the Crownsil of Twelve holds its meetings, as you will see. As indeed, Elroï, you have already seen."

Elroï!

Nothing of yesterday, then, had been a dream.

And——"Already seen"?

A dream and not a dream. What was real? Ellery thought in a detached desperation. He would ask no more questions. Listen, he told himself, listen. And observe. Perceive . . .

He perceived a hall running the length of the building, in the manner of the schoolhouse. It contained one very long and narrow table, with two benches of corresponding length along the sides, and two short benches, one at the head, the other at the foot. The only lamp he had yet seen in Quenan burned in a bracket over a door set in the far wall opposite the entrance—here evidently was the explanation for the kerosene the Teacher had bought at the End-of-the-World Store. End-of-the-World . . . If the world's end was anywhere, it was here in the Valley of Quenan surrounded by the hill called Crucible.

The old man was speaking again, pointing with his staff in the dim, yellowish, faintly flickering light. The doors in the long walls to the left and right led to sleeping quarters, he explained; the single door in the left wall led to his chamber, which was as large as the two rooms beyond the two doors in the right wall. And the patriarch went to the right wall and knocked with his staff on one of the two doors.

It was opened immediately by a young man, a very young man; eighteen, nineteen, Ellery thought, no older. A teen-ager with the face of a Michelangelo angel, except that it was rimmed by a crisply curling young beard.

The angelic face lit up with joy.

"Teacher!" he exclaimed. "When my brothers ran from the schoolhouse to tell me you had declared a holiday, and why, I put on my robes." He was dressed in a garment much like the old man's. "Guest"—he turned to Ellery and took both Ellery's hands in his—"Guest, you are welcome here. You are very welcome. Blessed is the Wor'd."

Ellery looked into his eyes, dark in the sun-browned young face; and the dark eyes looked back at him with infinite trust. Such trust that, when the boy gently released him, Ellery turned away. Who am I, he thought, that I should be looked at with such trust . . . with such *love* . . .? Who am I—or who do they think I am?

"Elroï—Quenan—" the patriarch was saying, "this is the Successor."

Successor? Ellery wondered. To what? But then he realized that, as the old man uttered the word, it was capitalized. Successor to whom? Instantly he knew the answer. Successor to the old man himself.

"Teacher, you called him . . ." The young Successor hesitated. "You called the Guest . . .?"

"By his names did I call him, Successor," said the old man gravely. "By his name which is Elroï, and by his name which is Quenan. It is he, Successor. It is indeed he."

At which the Successor, with a look of adoration, dropped to his knees, and prostrated himself, and kissed —yes, thought Ellery, it cannot be said any other way— kissed the hem of his garment.

"The room where I rest and sleep is the room next door. But this room," the Successor was saying (while Ellery reproached himself: *Why didn't I stop him? Why didn't I at least ask what it all means?*), "this room is where I study and write." He emphasized the last word slightly. "There is no other room like this one. It is called the scriptorium."

On the table were paper, ink, pens. As to what he might be writing, the Successor did not say.

The Teacher pointed with his long staff to the door under the lamp. "That room is the smallest," he said. "But the least shall be the greatest. That is the—" he pronounced a word. It sounded like "sanctum."

Sanctum? The holy place? Again Ellery could not be sure of what he had heard, again it seemed to him that there had been a pause, a hesitation . . . *sanc'tum.*

The dreamy haze, half mystification, half fatigue, through which he had been seeing everything, lifted for a moment. He heard himself asking matter-of-factly, like the Ellery Queen of a million years ago, "How do you spell that?"

"It is the forbidden room," said the Successor. Then, "Spell—? I will write it for you." The young man seated himself at a writing desk, selected a reed pen, fixed its point with a small knife, dipped it in a jar of ink, and wrote on a scrap of paper. There was something arcane, hieratic, about his manner. Scriptorium . . . Suddenly Ellery realized what it was: with his own eyes, in the century of rocket experimentation and quantum physics, he was actually beholding a scribe at work in the manner of the ancients. In silence he picked up the piece of paper.

Sanquetum.

That explained the pronunciation.

Which explained nothing.

"It is time, Teacher," Ellery said, "that you tell me just how your community is ruled. I must ask about other things, too. But that will do for the beginning."

The old man looked into him—past him, perhaps. "What you require of me, Quenan, I shall do, although I know that you ask only to prove me. We are not ruled, Quenan. We have no rule here. We have governance."

Something flashed through Ellery's mind; eluded him; then he had it. Some lines from an old book: *Dr. Melancthon said to Dr. Luther, Martin, this day thou and I will discuss the governance of the universe. Dr. Luther said to him, Nay, Phillip—this day thou and I will go fishing, and leave the governance of the universe to God.*

What Dr. Melancthon had replied, Ellery did not remember. "Fish, or cut bait," perhaps.

"Governance, then," said Ellery. The old man glanced at the Successor, who immediately rose and parted from them with a vigorous handclasp and a radiant smile.

Taking Ellery into the long hall, the Teacher seated him at the table of the Crownsil and sank onto the bench opposite. For a moment he seemed to meditate (or pray?). Then he began to speak. And as he spoke, Ellery felt himself slip back into the dream, the timeless world which possessed "what the world had lost." And the old one's voice was as soft as the lamplight on his face, which made Ellery blink, for it was like looking at a very old painting through a golden haze.

"The Crownsil of the Twelve," said the venerable Teacher, "I shall list for you in an order, Quenan. But in this order none is first, as none is last."

And he uttered a word. Was the word "grower"? "Growther"? Ellery puzzled over it. But he could not decide.

The Grower, or *Growther,* it seemed, oversaw all the crops and what they entailed: choosing which plots were to be planted to corn, which to cotton, or flax, or beans, or melons, or whatever; directing how they were tended, and by whom; and how harvested, and when.

The Herder. The Herder's responsibility was the cattle, sheep, goats, donkeys, and fowl of the community (there were no horses in Quenan, the Teacher said; what purposes horses might have served were more easily and economically served by the donkeys). The Herder saw that the beasts were kept from the growing crops and the young trees; he saw to their pasturage, to their breeding, and to the care of their progeny. The Herder was also a man wise in the ills of animals, although his methods kept Quenan's livestock in such rude health that his veterinary skills were not often needed.

The Waterman. The very existence of the community depended on the Waterman's labors. It was the Waterman whose duty it was to keep in good repair the cisterns and catch basins where the scant rains were stored; who saw that the wells were clean, the all-important springs kept open. He attended to the small aqueduct; and he husbanded the water of the irrigation ditches, portioning out what was needed for drinking, cooking, and the communal laundry and bath.

The Miller. The Miller made use, when there was sufficient water, of a waterwheel to grind the community's grains and legumes and even pumpkins into meal and flour. When there was no water, the Miller put up his sails and harnessed the winds. And if neither water nor wind was available, he blindfolded beasts so that they might not grow dizzy, and he walked them round and round to turn the millstones.

The Potter. Crucible Hill contained no clay, but at a distance of less than a day's journey by donkey, there was a clay pit. The Potter and his assistant turned out and fired the simple utensils of the community's people, glazing them with salt from a nearby pan. The Potter also made some things apparently needed for religious purposes, but what these were the Teacher did not say.

And the *Slave*—

"The what?" cried Ellery.

"The Slave," replied the Teacher with a sigh.

"You practice *slavery?*" Ellery heard his 1944 voice demand. To the ears of Elroï-in-Quenan it sounded brutally harsh and accusing. For in a community that lived a life of near-Biblical primitivity, was it so remarkable—?

"We merit your reproaches," the patriarch said humbly. "Yet surely it is known to you that we no longer number slaves among us? This is the last. He is in his eighty-eighth year."

"Resting from his labors, no doubt." First the display of bucolic ethics, then this!

"The Slave does no labor at all," the Teacher said.

"He serves only by membership in the Crownsil. His needs are cared for by us all."

"Decent of you," muttered Ellery-1944.

"In expiation. In community expiation."

And suddenly it occurred to Ellery that the community might be expiating not its own sins, but those of the nation. Was it possible this "Slave" was one of those who had been freed by the Proclamation or the 13th Amendment? Or was he a survivor of the Indian slavery that persisted in the remote Southwest for a decade or so longer?

It was likelier, Ellery thought, that he represented some dark chapter in the history of Quenan.

Quenan.

What the devil did the name signify? What language had it come from?

Ellery-1944 grew tired again in the slumbering air and dimness of the building. But the other Ellery—the Elroï—said softly, chin propped in both hands, "Go on Teacher. Please."

"Next is one whom you have already met."

The Storesman, to whom Ellery had lent his watch, was custodian of community property. Surrounded by the handmade things of his people, Storicai had taken childlike delight in something of alien manufacture.

The Chronicler. He kept the history, the records, the calendar, the genealogies, and the books of the community. The books consisted mainly of prayers, and these books the Chronicler maintained and repaired.

The Carpentersmith. In charge of all construction, maintenance, and repair of buildings, furniture, vehicles, and tools.

The Weaver. This office was currently held by a woman, although it was open to men also. Ellery thinking of Quenan in terms of ancient patriarchal societies, was surprised to learn that women were eligible for all offices.

The Elders. These were two, a man and a woman; each had to be at least seventy-five years old. They represented the special interests of the community's aged.

All matters of community welfare and policy were in the hands of this Crownsil of the Twelve. In any case requiring trial, they served as jury.

"To the Twelve, and to three others—myself as the Teacher, and to the Successor, and to the Superintendent—and to no others," said the old man, "belongs the right of entrance into this Holy Congregation House." He and the Successor lived there, and the Superintendent—whose duties, Ellery gathered, resembled those of a steward, or sexton—acted as liaison between the Teacher and the Crownsil.

"But to two alone belongs the right of silent entrance," said the Teacher. "These are your servant and his Successor."

"Your servant . . ." The dream was multiplying. Ellery felt like seizing his head in his hands out of sheer frustration. After all, *he* had been given entrance. Who in God's name was he supposed to be? Who was "Elroï Quenan"? To cover his confusion, Ellery repeated, "Silent entrance?"

The old hand—bone and vein and skin and sinew—gestured. "There is only one door into the holy house," he said. "That one through which we came. It is never locked; it has no lock. For this house is the heart of the Congregation." His voice did not rise; but it deepened with the fervor of belief.

In the language of modern anthropology, the house had *mana,* and as such it was *taboo* to the community. The only exceptions were rigidly fixed: the members of the Crownsil and the Superintendent. And even they were subject to a ritual discipline. Any of these wishing entrance must first sound the bell outside the door. Only if the Teacher himself answered might the official enter. If the Teacher was absent, or if he was engaged in prayer or meditation or study and did not reply to the bell, then he who rang had either to wait or to seek admittance at another time.

"For none but your servant—" (there it was again! *Is thy servant a dog, that he should do such a thing?* as practice slavery, for example? Was he being gently chided?) "—your servant or the Successor may be alone in this holy house," the old man explained. "To this rule we hold most strictly, as an outward sign of obedience to our holy regimen, that none may set foot in this house when I am not in this house, save only the Successor."

Ellery's weariness kept him from uttering the *Why not?* in his thoughts. Probably the old man himself could not give a reason. It was the Rule, the Law; all ritual hardened into that.

Ellery's glance wandered to the far end of the long hall, where stood the closed door with its overhanging kerosene lamp, the door to the room the youngster with the angelic face had called the "sanquetum."

At Ellery's glance, the Teacher said softly, "And the sanquetum. Yes. The forbidden room, as the Successor and the community commonly name it . . ."

Concerning this forbidden room, the old man went on to say, the rule was even stricter. Only one person in the community, the Teacher, might ever set foot in that room; not even the Successor might enter there. It was kept always locked, and the only key to the lock was held by the Teacher. (This was by contrast with the scriptorium, the Successor's official workroom; the door to the scriptorium might be locked, but it need not be, and to this door the Successor usually kept the only key.)

"Thus you see," the Teacher summed up, "our governance is by the fifteen elect: the Crownsil of the Twelve, and the Superintendent, and the Successor, and he who is the leader and the guide and the healer of his flock— thy servant, called the Teacher."

In Ellery's dream it came to him in an enormous waxing of light, like a sunburst, that he was not listening to a recital from some old and forgotten romance, but to the description of an actual community existing in the United States of America in the year 1944, apparently to the complete ignorance of county, state, and federal officials and to some 135,000,000 other Americans.

Searching his memory for a parallel, he could find only one: that tiny community, on its Appalachian mountaintop, which—isolated by a landslide that destroyed its only road to the outside world—remained forgotten for almost a generation, until communication was re-established.

But that had come about through an act of nature, and it had lasted only a short time in the scheme of things. On the other hand, no act of nature could explain Quenan; and from what Ellery had seen and heard, it had been here—isolated by choice—for a very long time. Storicai, the Storesman, had been awed by an automobile; he had apparently never seen nor even heard of a wrist watch.

How long? Ellery wondered.

And, quite mechanically, it became in his thoughts: *How long, O Lord?*

"Then nobody here owns anything?" Ellery asked. He had lost track of time; inside the hall of the Holy Congregation House, the flickering yellow light; outside, from time to time a voice—the soft moan of a cow, the two-note bray of a donkey—all without urgency or clamor.

"No," said the patriarch, "all belongs to the community."

Someone far inside Ellery's head remarked, *But that's communism*. Not the savage, specious communism of Stalinist Russia, but the freely willing way of the early Christians, and of . . . He struggled with the name; it was a pre-Christian group he had read about years before in Josephus. But he could not recapture it.

It was not really necessary to go back so far in time, he thought, or so far away in space. The American continent had a long history of such experiments. The eighteenth-century Ephrata Cloisters—"The Woman in the Wilderness," in Pennsylvania; the Zoarite community of east-central Ohio, which lasted forty-five years; the Amana Society—"The Community of True Inspiration"—founded near Buffalo in 1843, and still flourishing in Iowa in seven incorporated villages; the Shaker communal societies, remnants of which remained after more than a century and a half; the Oneida Community of "Perfectionists." These groups shared at least two common denominators: they were nearly all founded on a religious base, and in them all possessions were owned by all.

So, apparently, in Quenan. Its religious origin and nature, although they eluded Ellery, were evident; and— "all belongs to the community," as the Teacher said. As individuals its people owned nothing; whatever they grew or made, whatever service they performed, was contributed to and shared by and done for the benefit of all. In return, every Quenanite, young or old, strong or weak, received the portion of his need.

But what was "need"? And how draw the line between need and wish? Ellery saw vaguely that to hold this line it would be necessary to maintain absolute isolation from the world outside. A man could not covet something the very existence of which was unknown to him. And to guard against the nomadic nature of the human mind, which knew no boundaries, a system of indoctrination had to be basic to the community's way of life.

Pursuing this thought with the Teacher, Ellery learned that membership in the community came automatically with birth into it. There were no proselytes in Quenan, to spread the taint of civilization. Nor was there a period of probation, for if a probationer were to fail, what would become of him?—he could not be permitted to leave Quenan even under an oath of silence; suppose he were to break his oath and bring the world down upon them? So it was better not to admit the possibility of exclusion to begin with. As soon as the child in Quenan was old enough to enter the school, the Teacher exacted in the most solemn ceremony the child's vow of utter consent to the ways and laws of the community, with its primitive life, its isolation, its customs and hard labor and equal opportunities—and the sharing of all by all.

But this was merely the ritual that sealed the practice. "Give us the child for eight years," Lenin had said to the Commissars of Education in Moscow, "and it will be a Bolshevist forever." Hitler was proving the same thing with his parent-spying youth organizations. *Train up a child in the way he should go*—the scribes of Proverbs had noted twenty-three hundred years ago—*and when he is old he will not depart from it.* A Quenanite would no more question the nature of the community in which he had been rigidly reared and indoctrinated than a fish would question the nature of the sea in which it swam.

And it was of corollary interest to note that while there was the Weaver in this council, and the Herdsman, and the Carpentersmith, and the rest, there was no minister of war or defense, there were no police . . .

"I beg your pardon," Ellery said, "I'm afraid I did not quite catch that. How many did you say was the number of your people?"

"There are two hundred and three," the Teacher said. "The Potter's father ceased a week ago, but an elder sister of the Successor gave light to a girl-child three days since, so the number stands."

The sun sets, but the sun also rises.

In Quenan the sun rose on a communal dining hall, on even a communal bath, open at different hours for men and for women. Bathing, it appeared, was of more than mere hygienic importance here, although bodily cleanliness was a strict rule. In Quenan, as in primitive societies throughout time, bathing was also a ritual act, since what was bathed was the divine image which is man. When the Quenanites washed, they prayed; when they prayed, they washed. The washing of the body was an act of worship; worship, an act of cleansing.

"You prayed, too, I noticed, while we were eating," Ellery said.

"So do we all. For from our bread and wine we draw the strength to do the will of the Wor'd, and it is fitting that we bless the Wor'd as we eat. And we bless the Wor'd also for holy days and fast days, for festal days and for work days, for sunrise and sunset, for the phases of the moon and the seasons, for the rain and for the dry, for the sowing of the seed and the harvest of the crops—for all beginnings, for all endings. Blessed is the Wor'd."

Each male Quenanite was expected to marry by the age of twenty. If he failed to do so, the Crownsil, with the consent of all concerned, chose a wife for him; and the system seemed to work. Dr. Johnson, Ellery reflected, would have been pleased. The Great Cham had remarked once that he thought marriages would work out just as well if they were made by the Lord Chancellor.

One fact of life in Quenan, said the Teacher, made necessary a departure from the marriage-at-twenty rule. Because there was a slight preponderance of women in the community, females were granted an extra four years. If they were not married by the age of twenty-four, they became the wives of the Teacher. The Teacher explained this calmly.

"Men may sometimes be ill content if another man has more than they," he observed. "But in Quenan the Teacher is not as other men. This all believe, so all are content."

Ellery nodded. The Teacher, he supposed, was primarily a spiritual authority; the sacred office would transcend the man. As for the women who became his wives, they would be held in special esteem by the community, and probably they considered themselves fortunate—wasn't it Bernard Shaw who said that any intelligent woman would rather have a share in a superior man than the whole of an inferior one?

Ellery could not help wondering if, at his advanced age, the Teacher was still virile, like Abraham. Or did his young wives serve as mere bed-warmers against the chill of the night, as in the case of old King David? For that matter, how was it that so healthy a community remained so small in numbers? Continence? Control? Contraception? He wanted to ask, but he did not.

"You teach," he said instead. "What kind of textbooks do you use?"

"There is—" The old man paused. Then he resumed: "There is among us in common use one book only. It is our text in the school, it is our every family's prayer-book. The manual of understanding, some call it. The manual of knowledge, others say. Or the book of light, or the book of purity—of unity—of wisdom. Many are the names, one is the Book. It is the Book copied by the Successor in his scriptorium and kept repaired by the Chronicler in his library. It is the Book I have always with me."

He reached into his robe.

"Why, it's a scroll!" Ellery exclaimed.

"It is the Book." Carefully the Teacher unrolled a section of it.

Ellery recognized the Successor's handwriting. It was an odd script—odd as the local accent was odd. It was unlike any standard American penmanship—assuming such a thing to exist—that Ellery had ever seen. Was there a resemblance to the obsolete "Chancery hand" once used in certain English legal documents? He could not be sure. He also thought he detected the influence of some non-Western alphabet. Like so much else in Quenan, it was half revealed, half concealed.

for the pasture and for the sunlight on the pasture, we bless the Wor'd. may our hands work well and our feet walk well, in the pasture, and in coming, and in going. let us not lift up our voices in anger when we work or when we walk, not against brother, not against beast or bird, think on the Wor'd who keeps our voices from anger.

"I see," Ellery murmured. "I see . . ."

The prayers were written on small lengths of paper, each sewn with thread to the next until a considerable scroll was formed, and the whole rolled up and tied with a soft cord. There were no capital letters in the written text—this caught his attention at once—except the W of Wor'd . . . Yes, definitely a W. Did this mean that he had been wrong in thinking "Wor'd" was a corruption of "Lord"? Or had a simple pronunciation change come to reflect itself in the spelling? Or did the break in the word—indicated in the written form by an apostrophe, in the oral form by a just perceptible pause—

trace to a missing or dropped letter? And if so, did "Wor'd" stand for "World"?

Language, accents, attitudes, forms . . . So many things in Quenan (the name itself!) tantalized with their almost-differences. It was . . . yes, it was exactly like a dream, in which the powerless dreamer never quite grasped (while wholly grasping) the phantom realities of the experience.

Ellery looked up from the scroll. When he and the Teacher had sat down, what sunlight penetrated to the interior of the Holy Congregation House had come through the eastern windows. Now it was slanting through the western windows.

"It is no longer my custom to eat the midday meal," the Teacher said presently. "The people have finished theirs, but there is always enough for one more. Will you come now and eat? I will remain with you."

"I'm sorry that I've missed joining with the people." Ellery rose, feeling hunger. And, as always these days, weariness.

"There will be a time." The Teacher rose, too, and smiled. It seemed to Ellery a sad smile.

They paused outside the door. Ellery blinked and sneezed in the bright afternoon.

"This is the bell?" he asked. "The bell which must be rung and answered before entering the holy house?"

The Teacher nodded. The bell was perhaps a foot high. It was discolored with age, its surface scarred inside as well as out; the rim, where the clapper touched it, was worn very thin. It hung about chest-high; and by peering closely Ellery could see that two legends ran along its lip. One read:

17 The Foundary Bell Lane Whitechapel *21*

and the other:

From Earth's gross ores my Tongue's set free
To sound the Hours upon the Sea

An English-made ship's bell dating from the reign of Queen Anne! When this bell had been cast, the King James Bible was a mere century old; Shakespeare had walked the crooked streets of London during the childhood of some very old man; George Washington's birth was twenty years in the future. Through what perilous seas forlorn had the bell sounded its note through the centuries? And how (most marvelous of all) had it come here, to Quenan, in the American desert?

Ellery asked the Teacher, but the patriarch shook his head. As it was, so had it been. He did not know.

And, duly, Ellery marveled and went on to feed his stomach. The communal dining hall was like a barn with many windows, full of light and air and hearty smells. The food was simple and filling—a vegetable soup, chili and pinto beans, steamed corn with butter, stewed fruit, and another variety of herb tea. A young married couple waited on them; apparently this was a rotational duty. Wide-eyed, reserved, yet shyly expectant, with proper deference toward the Teacher, they gave most of their attention to the guest, the outsider. The only outsider they had ever seen.

Throughout Ellery's meal the Teacher prayed silently.

When Ellery was finished, the Teacher led him outside; and for the remainder of the afternoon—until the shadows inundated the land and the windows began to sprout candles—the old man conducted him about the Valley, answering Ellery's questions. Up and down the inner rim of Crucible Hill they went, surveying the cultivated fields, greeting the people at their toil. Ellery was fascinated. He had never seen so many different shades of green in a state of nature. And everything was aromatic with growing things and sagebrush smoke—the wood of the sagebrush was brought in from the desert hills, the Teacher told him, to feed the fires of Quenan ...

The dream quality intensified; in one day the world outside had become invisible in the mists, and the mists themselves had almost been forgotten. It was as if Quenan and all that it contained, including himself, *were* the world. (Had Adam and Eve known the nature of their Garden until they were cast out of it?)

On his curious sublevel the old Ellery kept musing. Where were art, and music, and literature, and science in this capsule in space-time? They were not here. But also not here—so far as he could tell—were discontent, and hatred, and vice, and greed, and war. The truth, it seemed to him, was that here in the lost valley, under the leadership of the all-wise patriarch, existed an earthly Eden whose simple guides were love of neighbors, obedience to the law, humility, mercy, and kindness.

And, above all, faith in the Wor'd.

It was late that night when Ellery finally voiced the question he had struggled with from the beginning.

They stood in the open doorway of the Holy Congregation House, with the soft uproar of the night in their ears. A sweet odor rose from the damp earth, resting from the day. The small glow of the lamp over the sanquetum door shone behind them in the quiet building.

"You are troubled, Elroï," the Teacher said.

"Yes," said Ellery. "Yes . . . It seems so long ago that we met. But it was only yesterday, at sunset, on the crest of the hill."

The Teacher nodded. His remarkable eyes pierced the darkness as if it were not there.

"You spoke then as if you had been expecting me, Teacher."

"That is so."

"But how could you have known I was coming? I didn't know it myself. I had no idea I was going to take the wrong turn—"

The Teacher said, "It was written."

So might a priest of the Toltec have answered Cortés, thought Ellery; and instantly wondered why the thought had come to him. Cortés, whose armor glittered like the sun god whose return had been predicted. Cortés, who had brought to the faithful of Quetzalcoatl only death and destruction. Ellery stirred.

"You spoke, Teacher," he said cautiously (was it out

of some atavistic fear that he might unleash evil merely by speaking of it?), you spoke of a great trouble that would befall your Valley and your people. And you said that I was sent to prepare—"

"To prepare the way. Yes. And to glorify the Wor'd."

"But what trouble, Teacher? And where is it written?"

The patriarch's eyes rested on him. "In the Book of Mk'h."

"I beg your pardon?" Ellery said. "The Book of what?"

"The Book of Mk'h," the Teacher said. "The Book which was lost."

A little drawer opened somewhere in Ellery's head: the fact that the Book *was* lost and not *is* lost was noted and filed away. "Mk'h . . ." he said. "May I ask how that word is spelled, Teacher?"

The old man spelled it, having some difficulty with the hesitation sign. "Mk'h," he said again, stressing the hesitation.

"Mk'h." Ellery repeated. "What does it mean, Teacher?"

The patriarch said simply, "I do not know."

"I see." How could the old man not know? "In what language is it, Teacher?"

The old man said, "Neither do I know that."

This was awkward. And Ellery bent to the task, examining the mystery. Mk'h . . . Could it be, he thought suddenly, some pristine or even aborted form of Micah? The Book of Micah! Sixth of the books of the Minor Prophets in the Old Testament . . . Micah, who had prophesied that *out of thee shall he come forth unto me that is to be ruler in Israel; whose goings forth have been from of old . . . And this man shall be the peace . . .* ! But . . . "The Book which was lost"? Had the Book of Micah ever been "lost"? Ellery could not remember. It seemed unlikely, for surely . . .

"The Book of Micah," Ellery said to the Teacher.

In the night, in the doorway of the holy house, the old man turned to Ellery, and the yellow glow on the far wall turned his eyes to flame. But it was only an effect of the lamp. For the Teacher said in a puzzled way, "Micah? No. Mk'h."

Ellery gave it up (for now, he told himself, but only for now). And he said, "This great trouble, Teacher. Is it written what kind of trouble it will be?" He swallowed, feeling childish. "A crime, perhaps?"

He might have touched the old man with a red-hot iron. Agitation rippled over the ancient face as if a stone had been thrown into a pond. "A crime?" he cried. "A crime in Quenan? There has been no crime among us, Elroï, for half a century!"

Concerning doctrine or prophecy one might doubt, but Ellery could muster no reason for rejecting the patriarch's testimony on a matter of yea-or-nay fact involving his own Valley. Yet how was it possible for a community of men, women, and children to exist which had known no crime for almost two generations? Since the days of—who had been President then?—Harrison, was it, the stern and bearded Presbyterian warrior who had been a general in the Civil War? Or walrus-mustached Cleveland, whose Vice-President was a man named Adlai E. Stevenson? No matter; it was another world, an American time and way of life as different as in Byzantium under the Paleologi—while here in Quenan, life must have been exactly as today . . . and in all that time—no crime?

"If there has been no crime in Quenan in half a century, Teacher," Ellery said carefully, "then surely I may infer that half a century ago there *was* a crime?"

"Yes."

"Would you tell me about it?"

The old man, tall against his taller staff, stood looking past Ellery at the ghost of a cottonwood tree, but not as if he were seeing it.

"Belyar was the Weaver then, and he had finished weaving ten bolts of cloth for the Storesman's shelves. But first Belyar cut from each bolt an arm-long length and concealed the ten lengths in his house, and he made for himself new garments out of them. The Storesman observed this, and examined the bolts, and he saw that they were not of the usual lengths; and he questioned him.

"Belyar was silent. This the Storesman reported to me, and I—when the Weaver again would not answer —I reported it to the Crownsil. It was a hard time. Much was considered. But at last a search was ordered; and in the presence of witnesses the Superintendent searched the Weaver's quarters and found scraps of the newly made cloth hidden in the bed, for the foolish man had not been able to part with even the scraps. And Belyar was tried by the Crownsil and he was declared guilty. Belyar's beard was brown and, as he worked much in the weaving shed out of the sun, his skin was very pale."

The sudden intrusion of this bit of description made Ellery start. He looked closely at the old man and thought he understood. That through-seeing gaze was looking at events happening again, happening now.

"He then confessed. 'The washing goes slowly,' Belyar said. 'And it is hateful to me to wear clothes which are not fresh and clean. I took what is mine by right. For it was the work of my own hands.'"

The heretic. One in fifty years!

"The Crownsil found him guilty, but it might not pass sentence. That heavy duty is the task of the Teacher. It was from my lips, then, that Belyar the Weaver heard his punishment for breaking the law of the community. I declared that he be given a piece of silver, and food and water sufficient for two days' sustenance, and that he be then driven into the desert, never to return on pain of death."

A piece of silver? It was the first mention of money Ellery had heard in Quenan.

"Never to return on pain of death, Teacher?" he said. "And was not the decree—sending Belyar into the desert with food and water for only two days—tantamount to sentence of death?"

"That is as it may be." The old man's face was set in stone. Then it softened. "It was within my power to decree Belyar's death directly. Yet in my weakness I found that I could not. Such a thing had not happened in my lifetime."

He went on to say that only strict obedience to their laws kept them a community, and that once the Weaver had broken the law he could not be permitted to remain in Quenan; there was no room for one whose continuing presence would ever remind the people of his awful act in stealing from his brothers. Nor could he be sent out into the world, for fear that he might bring the world down upon them. Thus banishment to the desert and almost certain death.

"He did not come back, or try to come back? Was his body never found?"

The old man sighed. "He was not seen or heard of again. And since his banishment there has been no crime in Quenan." And he fell silent.

What had become of the pale-skinned thief? Did he stagger about the desert until he fell and died of hunger and thirst, to be covered by the shifting sands? Or had some Indian or desert rat killed him for the sake of his silver piece? It was even possible that he had been found in time by a *ranchero,* or that by some miracle of good fortune and hardihood he had made his way to one of the cities of the plain or the seacoast. And there he would have taken up his life—in the era of the Beef Trust and the Sugar Trust and the Robber Barons; in the days when "that dirty little coward that shot Mister Howard" was entertaining the customers of his Leadville gambling hell with the tale of how he, Robert Ford, had put a bullet from an improved Colt .45 clean through the head of "Mister Howard"—Jesse James; when every Western town was rimmed with cribs offering raw sex for sale along with rotgut whisky . . . How long would Belyar and his piece of silver have survived in such a civilization? How could life in the Garden of Eden have prepared him for it?

Death directly, Ellery mused, would have been far more merciful. But the old man could not have known that.

And . . . "there has been no crime in Quenan" since.

That was something to think about!

"Then what is this great trouble which is written?" Ellery asked.

"I do not know," said the Teacher. "It is not written what it is, only that it will come." And he sighed again, heavily. "Until your coming, Elroï, I had thought it might be fire, or flood, or a shaking of the earth, or drought, or a plague of locusts, or a great sickness. Now, with your talk of crime . . . Can it be? I ask, can it be the evil of man of which it is written?

"My heart is sore," the old man went on, staring into the darkness. "For, ask myself what I will, I cannot think of a crime to come so great as to be in the Book. What sin can occur in Quenan?" he cried. "Here there is no cause for envy or for greed. Even the thieving of Belyar the Weaver could not occur today, for our storehouse bursts with the fruits of our toil; so that, should a man wish for more than the common allotment, he has but to ask for it and it is given him freely. Hate? There is no hate in Quenan; if there were, surely the Teacher would know it. Adultery? In all our days not even an accusation of such has been brought against any man or woman among us. Slander? False pride? False witness? I tell you, these cannot be in Quenan.

"For we do not wait to obey our laws, we run to do so with joyous feet. Corruption? What should I, or the Successor, or the Superintendent, or any of the Crownsil or the people generally, be corrupted with, and to what purpose? What one has, all have. And as bribery cannot be, so extortion cannot be. Here in Quenan, authority is not abused, trust is not broken, uncleanliness does not outlast the moment; and we are so slow to anger that the cause for it would wither before ever the anger came.

"My heart is troubled, Elroï, that you should suspect us of a capacity for crime."

The majestic voice ceased, and once again the little noises of the night intruded. Ellery shook his head in the darkness. It was too good to be true. He wanted to accept it, but he could not. Why hadn't the Teacher mentioned the greatest crime of all? he thought as the old man reached past him, shut the door of the Holy Congregation House, then took his arm and urged him gently onto the hardpacked earth of the village street.

Was it that the very notion was foreign to him and his community, so that it would never even cross his mind? As, for example, the concept of war was so foreign to the Eskimo culture that the people of the farthest North had no word for it in their vocabulary?

"And yet," the Teacher said in the lowest register of his deep voice, "and yet you are here, Elroï, and for a purpose. That which has been written for all the days to come I may know not; but this I know—that which will be, will be. Blessed be the Wor'd for your coming. I am thankful even so."

The water from the rivulet stopped splashing in the darkness somewhere, began again farther away, an irrigation ditch had been shut off, and another opened. He sensed that the Teacher was walking him back to the house where he had been lodged during the first night.

"How many years, Teacher, has Quenan been here?" he asked.

"To the number of three generations."

"And you are very old. Can you remember when the community was founded?"

The Teacher was silent. When he spoke, his voice seemed faint. "Tomorrow is another day, Elroï. This is your house. The Wor'd sustain you."

Ellery half imagined that there was a very slight tremor in the old man's powerful handclasp.

Later, lying on his pallet, Ellery heard a frog in some ditch lift up its voice. *Weedit, weedit.* And then another, and another, and another. *Weedit, weedit, weedit . . .* Not more than half awake, Ellery thought of frog spawn, silent in still waters; then of tadpoles, still silent; then the swift ascension to the land, the swarming, the crawling, the croaking . . . and at the last a voice, a human voice, saying something stubbornly.

Nevertheless, this voice said, fading as Ellery sank into sleep, *the world does move . . .*

III

TUESDAY

April 4.

ELLERY WAS FINISHING his breakfast in the communal dining room when the interruption came. (In spite of stern intentions he had overslept, and he was alone in the building except for the commissary staff, who were quietly cleaning up around him. He had tossed on the pallet all night and regretted having neglected to take one of the red capsules from the little bottle in his grip. Also, he missed coffee. Herb tea might be wonderfully healthful, but it did nothing for the taut Queen nerves.)

The interruption came in the form of an excited voice.

"Quenan!"

The young man washing a nearby table top looked up, startled; then at Ellery, awed; then away.

"Quenan!" The voice was nearer. "Elroï—"

The Successor burst into the dining hall, his angelic face alight, the long hair tumbling into the curls of his young beard. "There is a message for you—" For a moment Ellery fancied that someone from outside had tracked him down—the mere possibility made him recoil. But then the Successor said, "—from the Teacher. He asks that you come at once to the holy house!" And the young man ran out.

Ellery jumped up and hurried out after him. But the young Successor was speeding off in another direction, evidently on some task or errand, and Ellery made his way quickly to the Holy Congregation House. Here, just as he was about to open the door, he remembered the taboo, and he took hold of the bellrope instead and pulled it twice. And waited.

Butterflies danced between the world of light and the world of shade. The sound of wood being chopped came to him: ka-thuh-*thunk*, ka-thuh-*thunk*. And the rich green smell of earth and water and plants.

Just as the door of the holy house opened, a little boy rode by astride the pinbones of a young donkey, intent on the dancing butterflies.

"Teacher—" Ellery said.

And—"Teacher," said the little boy.

And—"Blessed be the Wor'd," the Teacher said, to both. His eagle's face softened as he looked at the child, and he raised his hand in a graceful gesture of benignity. "Walk in beauty," the Navajo says in farewell. This old man walked in beauty.

The little boy smiled with delight. Then he spied Ellery, and the smile wavered. "Blessed be the Wor'd," the child lisped hastily, and with uplifted hand made the same gesture.

"Come," the old man said to Ellery. And he shut the door.

This time they did not sit at the table or pause at the Successor's empty rooms. The Teacher led Ellery to the only door of his own room. The light shed by the lamp over the sanquetum door in the main meeting room penetrated to the Teacher's chamber, with its few stark furnishings, and by itself would have served dimly to illuminate it; but the chamber contained its own arrangements for light. These were three tall, very narrow windows, scarcely more than slits a few inches wide, one set in the far wall opposite the door, the other two in the walls to the side. Through each of these slit-windows a plinth of sunlight entered, to meet in the exact center of the room at the bed standing there, so that the bed itself was bathed in sun. (And now Ellery realized that three walls admitting sunlight meant three *outside* walls; the Teacher's room was architecturally a wing of the building, exactly balanced on the other side by a wing housing the Successor's two smaller rooms.)

The Teacher's chamber was the room of a cenobite. Its narrow trestle bed was of wood covered by sewn sheepskins—its mattress—with a single thin blanket neatly spread out. To each side of the head of the cot stood a small square table; two rude chests occupied the midpoints of the two facing side-walls; a stool in one corner was identical with a stool in the corner diagonally opposite. The room itself was square.

And so it was easy, in this room of perfect balance, to sense that something was out of balance. Something jangled in this orderly structure, something was off-key.

Key . . . Ellery's eye leaped, just anticipating the Teacher's pointing finger, to the top of the left-hand table. On it, to one side and near a corner, lay a bracelet of some dull metal; and attached to the bracelet was a single key.

"Someone moved the key last night," the Teacher murmured. He saw that Ellery was puzzled, and he said, "For someone to enter my room without my knowledge —Elroï, this is a grave matter."

"How can you be sure," Ellery asked, "that the key was moved?"

The old man explained. Each night after saying his prayers he took off the bracelet and placed it in the exact center of the table top. "Symmetry," he said, "is a way of life with me, Elroï. I hold it the purest of esthetic forms."

This startled Ellery, who had seen no evidence of esthetic devotion in the village: beauty, yes, but unrealized. *Euclid alone looked on beauty bare . . .*

"—and when I awoke this morning, I found the bracelet where you see it now—not centered on the table, but near a corner. By this I know that someone entered my room as I slept. And what is far more serious—"

"—must have entered the holy house without ringing the bell, by stealth?" The Teacher nodded, fixing Ellery with his prophet's eyes. "This is not necessarily so, Teacher," Ellery said.

"How not? Though it is true that I am the lightest of light sleepers. Still, the bracelet has been moved. I can hardly count the years I have slept here, and nothing like this has happened before. Is it a sign? A warning?"

Ellery looked around, studied each of the slat-thin windows in turn. "No one could have come through one of these," he said, "not even the smallest child. But someone could have *reached* through . . . with a fishing rod—No," seeing the incomprehension on the old face, "no fishing rod here. All right—a pole, then, a long stick of some sort. With it, someone could have lifted the bracelet from the table, pulled it through the window, and later returned it the same way."

"But why?" asked the Teacher, in the same troubled way.

Ellery picked up the key. It was crudely fashioned from the same dull metal as the bracelet. It looked rough and pitted, but it felt smooth—too smooth. Partly on impulse, partly because he had felt this smoothness on keys before, Ellery lifted it to his nose. That wild, pungent odor—

"Do you keep bees here?" he asked.

"Yes, although not many. We save most of the honey for the sick. And the wax—"

"Just so," said Ellery. "The wax."

Someone had taken a wax impression of the key during the night. And someone had fashioned, or was even now engaged in fashioning, a duplicate key—to what?

"This is the key to the sanquetum, the forbidden room. It is the only key, and I alone may have it, for I alone may enter. Not even the Successor may accompany me," the old man said. "Or have I told you that?"

They were silent. Voices faded down the lane, died away. A far-off cowbell sounded; an ass; the woodcutters broke their own silence: ka-thuh-*thunk*, ka-thuh-*thunk*. Somewhere children sang a simple song of a few pure notes. With such treasure as this, what was there to conceal in the sanquetum?

Ellery asked the question.

The old man sat down on one of his stools. Elbow on knee, hand on forehead, he pondered. At last he rose, beckoning Ellery to follow. They went out into the meeting room and stood together beneath the lamp burning over the locked door.

"It would be permitted for you to enter," said the Teacher, with some difficulty.

"Oh, no," Ellery said, very quickly.

"If you are here to open the Way, you may surely open this door."

But Ellery could not bring himself to the act. Whatever strange error had mistaken him for their Guest, to take advantage of it by setting foot in the holy of holies would desecrate it.

"No, Teacher. Or, at least, not now. But do you, please, go in. Look around with care. If anything is missing, or even out of place, tell me."

The Teacher nodded. From a niche in the wall he took a ewer and a basin and a cloth and washed his hands and face and feet and dried them, murmuring prayers. His lips still moving, he unlocked the door. And in reverent silence, walking delicately, the old man entered the forbidden room.

Time passed.

Ellery waited in patience.

Suddenly the Teacher was back. "Elroï, nothing is missing from the sanquetum. Nothing is out of place. What does it mean?"

"I don't know, Teacher. But that someone has made a duplicate key to this holy room, I am sure. Obviously there is something in the sanquetum that one of your people wants. Tell me everything that is in the forbidden room. Leave nothing out."

The lids came down over the black-blazing eyes as the old seer looked into his memory.

"There is a tall jar containing scrolls of prayers. There is another jar containing scrolls of prayers. There is the holy arque in which the Book of Mk'h is kept—"

"The book—"

"—and the front of this arque is of glass. And there is also the treasure."

"What treasure?" Ellery asked slowly.

The old man's eyelids opened; Ellery could see the pupils widen as they were exposed to sudden light.

And he said, "The silver.

"And now the time has come, Elroï Quenan, for me to answer the question you were about to ask last night. Let us seat ourselves at the Crownsil table."

It was The Year of the First Pilgrimage, a name not given to it until much later. The Teacher was then a youth living with his father and mother in San Francisco, but not happily. The friends who shared their faith were equally unhappy.

On the one hand, the city (or so it seemed to him) was seething with sin. Drunkards reeled down the hilly streets; their obscenities fouled the air. Saloons stood on every street corner, ablaze with gaslight and noisy with cheap music to tempt the weak and unwary. Gambling dens swallowed the money needed to feed men's children, families were made paupers overnight. Dishonesty was the boasted rule in commerce; the few who refused to cheat went to the wall, without credit from the coarse multitude for even the honesty that had put them there.

No man's son was proof against the temptations of the vile Barbary Coast, which made of the human body an article of commerce. Even though shame, disease, and death lurked like jungle beasts, no man could be sure even of his own daughter.

Was not the whole city a gaudy sink? Was not the whole country?

A farmer or rancher might feel safe from the distant corruption; he soon felt the pain of nearer ills. He found himself slave to the railroad, whose unchecked tolls robbed him of most of his profit; the plaything of speculators, who juggled the prices his produce sold for.

While in the nation's capital a man of war—said to be a drunkard—sat in the highest office of the land! Political places were bought and sold by his lieutenants without scruple. Huge corporate combines, with the connivance of his administration, scandalously plundered the people's resources.

It was a black time for the God-fearing. Where to turn? Where to go?

The self-contained world of the Latter-Day Saints seemed to offer a way and a destination; but it was open only to those who professed the Mormon faith. And this, for the Teacher's people, was impossible.

Ellery leaned forward eagerly. "Why, Teacher?"

"Because of our own faith," replied the old man.

"Yes, of course. But what is it? Where did it come from?"

The Teacher shook his Biblical head. The roots of Quenan's faith, he said, went so deep into the past that not the oldest member of the holy community—even in the Teacher's childhood—could say whence it grew. It could be traced through many generations and countries, but the trail became fainter and more difficult to follow, until at last it vanished altogether in the wilderness of time. Communicants had fallen by the wayside, but always a small hard core of the faithful remained to keep the faith alive.

Ellery's persistent questions turned up little. The Bible apparently played no direct role in the beliefs of the Teacher's people, although it colored their traditions and theology. The sect (if that was what it was) had once had a way of life, it appeared, that had been "lost" in the long march of the centuries; the tradition of this vanished way of life had been handed down from Teacher to Teacher, the old man said, and he made a vague reference to the pages of Pliny and Josephus (there it was again, Ellery thought suddenly—a confirmation of his own fugitive recollection).

In sum, the Teacher continued, the Crownsil of his youth in a series of solemn meetings made a decision: They must leave the abominable world in which they found themselves. Somewhere in the vast lands to the east, even if in desert wastes, their people would seek a place in which they might live, uncontaminated, as a self-contained community, in strict accordance with their own ethical and socio-economic principles.

And so the people sold their houses and lands and businesses; wagons and supplies were purchased; and one day a great caravan left San Francisco and began the eastward trek. And this was another long, hard time.

Their first attempt at settlement, on a verdant tract of land not far from Carson City, was disastrous. They had chosen the site because there was then no railroad to the Nevada capital and, compared with San Francisco, Carson City was a mere village. But its very smallness proved their undoing. Saloons and gambling hells and dance halls, because of the lesser scale of Carson City, proved too tempting to many who had been frightened off by the massive bawdiness of the great city on the Bay. And the strange ways of the colony brought them unwelcome visitors, who came to stare and jeer, men of foul mouths accompanying birdlike flocks of gaudy-plumaged, shrieking women.

Within a year the Crownsil decreed the Carson City colony a failure; they must move on. Most of their worldly assets were tied up in the land purchase and must be written off; very well, they would go where money was not merely unnecessary, but useless. They would find a place so remote, so off the beaten track, that the world would forget them—would not even know of them.

Through many nights and days thereafter, the caravan toiled southeast. People died and were buried by the wayside. Young men and women were married. Children were born.

Generally, the migration tried to avoid settlements. It happened once, however, that a man died after having been taken to a doctor in a frontier village. He had no family, and no one could be spared to drive his wagon, nor was there any room for his goods and gear in any of the other wagons. So everything was sold in the village for fifty silver dollars, and the wagon train moved on— not, however, before attempts were made to seduce several of the girls, to rob the Teacher's father of the fifty silver dollars and the rest of the wagon train's dwindling cash, to entice one couple into claiming the teams and wagons of the entire colony with promise to support the dishonest claim by perjured evidence and a venal judge and jury. All these attempts failed. The latter-day pilgrims left town with dogs turned on them, stones thrown, and guns fired to stampede their beasts.

It was their last contact with civilization.

Food was running low and water had run out when the tugging of their oxen, smelling the springs, brought the pioneers to the ringed hill which they were to call Crucible. Here was a veritable oasis in the desert, hidden, green, rich in water and arable soil, with space enough to grow food for all their number. And they called the valley Quenan.

(Ellery, thinking about this later, decided that "Quenan" might be a corruption of "Canaan," altered by the local accent and grown pronouncedly different in isolation. Though they might not possess a single copy of the Bible, the noble language of the King James Version was familiar to all nineteenth-century Americans: what more natural than that, consciously or otherwise, they should have identified their wanderings in the wilderness with those of the Children of Israel? So he was to think, but he was never to be sure.)

In the Valley they settled, building their first rude shelters from the wood and canvas of the wagons; and here they had remained ever since.

The exodus from San Francisco must have taken place in 1872 or 1873; from Carson City in 1873 or 1874.

"And in all these years," Ellery asked incredulously, "no stranger has ever found his way here?"

The Teacher reflected. "I believe I said earlier that

that was so. But I had forgotten—there was one. It came to pass some forty years ago, during one of the Potter's journeys with his assistants into the desert to obtain the special clay of which our prayer-scroll jars are made. A man was found lying in the sands; it was far north of Quenan. The man barely breathed. We hold life sacred; and in spite of our laws the Potter brought him here and he was nursed back to health. As it turned out, no harm was done, for his ordeal in the desert had erased from his mind all memory of the past, even his name. So we instructed him in our faith and our laws, and he lived in Quenan as one of us for the rest of his days. I had lost the habit of thinking of him as from the outside. He ceased some years ago."

One intruder in seventy years, and that one a blank page! Did the community know anything of the world outside? Very little, apparently. Once in a great while the Teacher or the Storesman saw, at or near Otto Schmidt's store, a wagon which needed no beasts to pull it, like Elroï's own; and, of course, for some years the people had caught occasional glimpses of flying machines that made a noise like distant thunder in the sky; but as to events . . . The old man shook his head. Even he, the Teacher, the oldest and most learned man in the Valley, knew nothing of the outside; nor did he wish to know.

"Do you remember the Civil War?" Ellery asked.

The sun-black forehead creased. "That would have to do with"—he paused, as if the next word were unfamiliar—"soldiers? Who wore clothes of blue? I was a young child . . . There is in my mind a confused recollection of many marching men in blue . . . many people shouting . . . my father's voice saying that these were soldiers coming back from the Rebellion . . ."

Of World War I the old man knew nothing. And it was clear that he was equally ignorant of the second global war in a generation, the one currently being waged. Had not Otto Schmidt mentioned it? But the old man shook his head. "I do not speak to him of worldly things; he thinks we are wild men, hermits, and knows nothing of our community. We revere truth, but Quenan must remain hidden from men's minds."

The Teacher showed no curiosity whatever about the war, and he seemed quite unconscious of the many United States laws he and his people were daily breaking, not to mention the laws of the state.

Such was the story as Ellery pieced it together from the Teacher's account and, later, from the scant records he was able to consult in the archives of the Chronicler . . .

It was while he pored over the Chronicler's records (his search for some reference in them to Josephus or Pliny was in vain, and the Chronicler had not even a dozing acquaintance with the names) that Ellery suddenly remembered. Both Josephus and Pliny the Elder had written of a religious order originating in the second century B.C. called the Essenes—yes, and now that he thought about it, so had the first century A.D. Jewish philosopher of Alexandria, Philo, who had also left an account of a non-Christian ascetic sect in the Egypt of his time whom he called the Therapeutae.

The Essenes had practiced strict communal possession; scrupulous cleanliness—the frequent ceremonial washings of the Quenanites? The Essenes had abhorred lying, covetousness, cheating; they subsisted by pastoral and agricultural activities and handicrafts.

Was it possible that the sect of Quenan had descended from the ancient Essenes? But there were important differences: the Essenes had abstained from conjugal relations; they had condemned slavery.

Ellery wondered. Practices, even beliefs, might well have been lost or modified in the course of over two thousand years by a people with poor written records and the pressures of dispersion in a swiftly proliferating world of Christians and Moslems . . . It was possible. But no one would ever know.

"Quenan must remain hidden from men's minds . . ." That is, the secret valley was a world unto itself, secure in its purity from outside contamination.

But now its purity was threatened by contamination from within.

Someone of the community had, by stealth and contrivance, made a duplicate of the Teacher's key to the sanquetum. Why? The reason must be an overpowering one. For the act was not only Quenan's first crime in almost two generations, but, unlike Belyar's theft of the cloth fifty years before, it was also an act of sacrilege.

Mere curiosity about the sanquetum—a perverse impulse to see the interior of the forbidden room simply because it was forbidden? Possible, but unlikely; in the face of a powerful taboo, curiosity alone would hardly induce a Quenanite to go fishing in the dead of night through one of the slit-windows in the room of the revered Teacher for the sanquetum key, to take a beeswax impression of it, to return the key, and then to manufacture a duplicate from the mold.

No, the act must have a more tangible base than that.

Theft? But of what? The jars of prayer scrolls? But every family had its own prayer scrolls. The holy book of—what had the Teacher called it?—Mk'h, "the book which was lost" but which, presumably, had been found again? This might be the reason if the community were torn by religious dissension—schism, heresy; but it was not.

That seemed to leave only the "treasure" of the silver coins—the fifty dollars realized by the Teacher's father from the sale of the goods of the man who had died on the trail after the community's exodus from Carson City, and which had apparently been hoarded as a sort of special fund, cash expenditures having been made out of the community's original paper money for as long as it lasted.

But what could anyone in Quenan want with fifty silver dollars, or even one silver dollar? Some bauble at Otto Schmidt's store? The forbidden pleasure of mere possession of the shiny coins?

Ellery shook his head. It was a puzzle—a deep puzzle.

The Teacher rose, staff in hand. His ancient face was

torn with grief. "I fear, Elroï, that this matter of the key may indeed be the beginning of the calamities which have been foretold. But now I must go to the children; they are awaiting me in the school. I go with a troubled heart."

"It may be, Teacher," Ellery said, rising also, "that you make too much of this." But his tone conveyed his own misgivings.

"It will be as it will be," the old man said. "You will find the Waterman on the south slope, waiting to show you the aqueduct and the irrigation canals."

And Ellery heard himself saying, "The Wor'd sustain you, Teacher."

The old eyes, which had as usual been staring through Ellery, narrowed and focused on him.

"Blessed be the Wor'd," said the Teacher.

IV

WEDNESDAY

April 5.

ELLERY DECIDED RATHER early the next morning that the Superintendent would have made the perfect minor civil servant anywhere in the overcivilized world. He had been designated by the Teacher to conduct the Guest to the northernmost part of the Valley and to point out to him those features of the Valley which they would encounter en route.

"I will conduct you to the northernmost part of the Valley," the Superintendent said to Ellery's Adam's apple in a sort of liturgical mumble.

"So the Teacher told me," Ellery said.

"And I will point out to you those features of the Valley which we shall encounter—"

"So the Teacher—"

"—en route," the Superintendent concluded. He was a shiny sort of man who looked as ageless as a robot. He might have been a postal inspector in Iowa or an assistant curator of a provincial Yugoslavian museum or a sealer of scales in a small municipality in Australia. Did the nature of the work produce this type, or did the type seek out the work? Ellery decided to be philosophical and make the best of it. He was stuck with the man for the whole morning.

"Let's go, then," Ellery said, stopping a sigh.

"Shall we go?" the Superintendent asked promptly. And after a few silent moments of walking he said, "That is the communal dining hall."

"I know, Superintendent. I ate there this morning. And yesterday. And the day before."

The man looked at him glassily. "It is where the community eats," he said.

"Ah," said Ellery. "Thank you." What was the use?

In the course of their tour his guide pointed out the laundry ("That is the laundry. Clothes are washed there"), the wool washery ("I will point out to you the wool washery. It is there. That is where we wash the wool"), the donkey stable ("—where donkeys are stabled"), an alfalfa field ("—field. Alfalfa is grown there. Animals eat it"), a peach orchard ("A peach orchard. On those trees peaches grow. They are good to eat"), and other landmarks of Quenan.

"And this is the northernmost part of the Valley. Here is the peaceful place."

"The peaceful place?" Ellery repeated, perplexed.

"The place of peace. It occupies the entire valleyside slope of the northern hill," the Superintendent explained, as if Ellery were stone-blind. Ellery decided to be charitable. After all, it *was* the first time in his life that the Superintendent had been called upon to fill the role of tourist's guide. "There are almost one thousand places here, Elroï. Or perhaps more than one thousand; early records are faulty. Each has the same stone. The dimensions of the stone are: at the base, one foot square; in height, two feet; at the top, three-quarters of a foot square."

"Do you mean—?"

"Each place at the top of the slope is six feet in depth, at the bottom five. The widths vary."

Ellery stood in silence.

A thousand headstones, each marked with the same

strange carving. As if a tree were to be reduced to its essential structure. There was no writing.

The wind sang in passing.

The Superintendent's flat voice took on a certain contour. "In the fifth row from the top, at the eleventh place from the right, lies my father, and seven places from him lies my mother," he said. "One row below and fifteen places from the right lie my wife and our child. And blessed be the Wor'd which sustains us all, here and forever."

He said no more words aloud, but Ellery saw that he was praying.

My wife, he had said. *Our child*. Not *my first wife*, or *our eldest child*, or *our youngest child*.

Time passed.

Ellery said, "I'm sorry." The words were not intended as a concession to death; they were an apology for having judged a man to be a robot.

Voices from below made him turn his head. Two figures were coming toward them, one slowly, one quickly; but the slower reached them first, having started sooner.

It was the guardian of the place of peace, a gnomelike old man with marked cretin features. His speech was too thick for Ellery to follow, but from the gleeful gestures of the small scythe in his blackened hand it appeared that he was describing his work in trimming the grass that grew upon the thousand graves. Was that pride shining from his dim eyes? Ellery felt his flewh crawl.

And the Superintendent said, "He does a work that must be done, and so he justifies his bread. Also, if he and the very few like him who are born to us teach us the love which is difficult, it cannot be said that they were born in vain."

The love which is difficult . . .

Once more Ellery said, "I'm sorry."

By now the second man had reached him.

It was the Successor, as it had been the previous morning.

And his message was the same.

The old Teacher said, "This morning the bracelet with the key was on the other side of the table."

Ellery examined the key again. It looked like something used for a medieval keep, for it was fashioned from a single huge slab of metal on one plane. It still smelled, though less strongly, of the dark and unbleached beeswax into which it had been pressed.

Suddenly the Teacher said, "You have seen something."

Ellery nodded. (A bit of nonsense jumped out of his memory: The old lady asking the storekeeper if he had a "signifying" glass, and at the storekeeper's negative, saying with a sigh, "Well, it don't magnify.")

He fished in his pocket for the powerful little lens he always carried with him, unfolded it, and looked intently through it at the key. Then he handed the lens to the old man.

"I see marks of a sort," said the Teacher. "Here, and here, and here on the edges of the bit. Scratches." He looked up. "I do not understand."

"File marks," Ellery said. "And fresh—they weren't there yesterday. It seems clear, Teacher, that whoever borrowed your key to the sanquetum and took a wax impression, for the purpose of making a duplicate key, found that his first work was faulty. Therefore he had to correct the fault. He worked on the duplicate key with a file, after fitting the duplicate over your key—this original—for guidance."

The old man seemed uncertain of his meaning. But Ellery had already left the Teacher's room and was striding toward the door of the sanquetum. The old man followed.

Ellery tried the door. "Locked," he said.

"As it should be."

Ellery stooped for a close look at the lock. "Will you observe this, Teacher?"

The old man stooped. By the lock were fresh scratches in the time-polished surface of the wood.

"It means," Ellery said, "that an attempt was made to

open the sanquetum door with a key that did not fit."

The old man shook his head. "I am confused," he confessed. "He who made the key worked over it with a file to correct it, and still the key did not fit?"

"You're reversing the probable order of events. It must have happened like this:

"Two nights ago, while you were asleep, someone reached in through one of your slit-windows with a long reed or pole, lifted the key ring off your table, took it away, and in a safe place made a wax impression of the key. The key itself he then returned to your table by the same method, not knowing that you always placed it in the mathematical center of the table top.

"From the wax impression he made a duplicate key, and with this duplicate he stole into the holy house last night and tried to unlock the door of the sanquetum. The duplicate key did not work.

"He realized that the copy he had made was not sufficiently accurate. But to correct it he needed your key again. Thereupon he stole out of the Holy Congregation House and around to one of the windows of your room in the wing, and with a pole or reed he again took possession of your key, and again he went off with it—this time to correct the inaccuracies in his duplicate with a file. He then returned your key on its bracelet to your table with his pole, once more failing to realize that it should be placed in the exact center of the table. Have you investigated the sanquetum, Teacher, to see if anything is missing this morning?"

"Nothing is missing," said the old man with difficulty.

"Then I suppose the coming of dawn or some other reason kept him from using the corrected key on the sanquetum door in the early hours of this morning."

The bearded face was set in a multitude of fine hard lines, like an etching.

"It is to be expected, then . . ." The words stuck in the old man's throat.

"I'm afraid so," said Ellery gravely, pitying him. "He will make another attempt to enter the sanquetum, undoubtedly tonight, and undoubtedly this time the duplicate key will work."

There was no one else in the holy house.

The Teacher had given grim assent to Ellery's request that he be permitted to examine the interior of the forbidden room alone. Then the old man had left, wrapped in silence, and since the Successor was off on an errand somewhere, Ellery had the sacred building to himself.

He found himself squaring his shoulders. If the leader of this curious flock permitted him to set foot in their holy of holies, why should he hesitate? Yet hesitant he did feel, as if he were about to commit sacrilege—a "profanation of the mysterie."

Still, it had to be done. He inserted the big key in the lock, felt the heavy tumblers turning over, pushed the door open, and stood on the threshold of the forbidden room.

It was really no larger than a large closet. There were no windows. The only light came from what he took to be an eternal lamp—an oddly shaped oil lamp of some time-crusted metal hanging from the precise center of the ceiling. The draft caused by the opening of the door had set the lamp in motion; it swung now, slightly, back and forth, like a censer, scattering shadows instead of smoke.

And in the shifting light Ellery saw:

To either side of him, each in a near corner, a very tall and slender jar of pottery, purple in color, resting on a wooden base and surmounted by a bowl-like cover. Jars, bases, bowls were identical.

Directly facing him: an old-fashioned walnut china closet, glass-fronted. On the bottom shelf lay a book, open. And on the upper shelf were two perfectly stacked columns of silver coins of equal height, in accordance with the fundamental principles of symmetry—"the purest of esthetic forms."

Nothing else.

When the eternal lamp had come to rest and his eyes

had grown accustomed to the light, Ellery removed one of the jar covers and looked in. It contained many rolled papers—scrolls—each secured with a bit of purple thread. He replaced the cover and looked into the other jar; it, too, was full of scrolls.

He turned his attention to the cabinet.

It reminded him so strongly of the china closet that had stood in his grandmother's dining room during his childhood that he half expected to find the shelves filled with the same blue-and-white willow-pattern dishes. But this one contained nothing except the open book and the two columns of coins. Through the glass front he studied the book. It seemed printed in the black-letter type called Old English (the phrase "Cloister Black" flickered in Ellery's memory), or at any rate in some font with a close resemblance to it. It was difficult to make out in the poor light, so Ellery put off for the moment the task of deciphering it and turned his attention to the two columns of coins. They were remarkably bright and shining.

He opened the china closet. Old silver dollars in mint condition!

He dipped into his store of numismatic knowledge. Some of the old "cartwheels," he recalled, were quite rare.

Was this the reason for the duplicate key and someone's plan to invade the sanctuary? Was the would-be thief concerned with the monetary value of the "treasure" of Quenan?

There was the almost legendary silver dollar minted in San Francisco in—when? yes!—1873, the same year the Quenanite sect had probably left that city in its quest for a new settlement. Only seven hundred had been minted, and all but the proof copies held by the mint had disappeared. Speculations about their fate had run from the theory that they had been buried somewhere and the secret of the hiding place lost through sudden death to the equally unprovable hypothesis that they had wound up in China as payment for lead-lined chests of green unfermented tea or even opium. But suppose everyone was wrong, and these—these two neat pillars of coins, as perfect as on the day they were minted—were the "lost" 1873 San Francisco dollars? A single specimen would be worth a fortune! And there were—how many?

With shaking fingers Ellery lifted one of the coins from the left-hand column and peered closely. The face of the coin depicted Liberty seated, and the date . . . *1873!* He turned it over, holding his breath. The obverse showed the American eagle ("a verminous bird," Ben Franklin had called it disdainfully, "a stealer of other birds' catches," in urging the adoption of the turkey as the national emblem instead). If there was an *S* below the eagle—signifying the San Francisco Mint . . .

Ellery took out his little magnifying glass and searched out the mint mark. Disappointment washed over him. It was not *S*. It was *CC*.

Of course—*CC*, Carson City. The capital of Nevada had had its own mint in those days, when a flood of silver poured out of the nine-year-old state's rich mines. And then as now Nevadans had favored hard coin over paper money . . . He checked the other coins. All bore the *CC* mint mark.

Ellery restacked them with great care in the same two perfect columns and closed the glass door of the china closet.

While not the priceless silver dollar of the 1873 San Francisco mintage, the 1873 *CC* was valuable enough. Each specimen, he guessed, would be worth about two hundred dollars now—perhaps more, considering their perfect condition. But again the question was: Who in Quenan would even think of stealing money? And what good would it do him if he succeeded? That the would-be thief had any knowledge of the coins' numismatic value he discounted at once. No, to the Quenanite thief the coins would have, at the most, their face value. And to steal a handful of dollars invested with the taboo of sacred objects . . . Ellery shook his head. Whatever value these coins represented to the thief, it was not material. But what? He could not even gsess.

He left the sanquetum, its shadows shifting weirdly with his movements, and locked and tried the door. Then he went seeking the Teacher at the school.

Gravely, Ellery returned the key.

"Where," he asked the old man, "is the Chronicler to be found?"

The Chronicler provided an antic note to Ellery's sojourn in the Valley. The old Quenanite sported a crop of curly, grizzled whiskers, rather short. No hair grew on his upper lip, which had sunken into his upper jaw from the long-time absence of incisors. This gave the lip a remarkable flexibility. He would suck it in with a rather startling noise, a combination *smack-click;* this caused his lower lip to shoot forward, so that the total effect was of a sort of spitting, intelligent old monkey. The old man's shoulders were frail and bowed; his head was bald except for a matted gray fringe, like a tonsure. I know, Ellery thought suddenly: he looks like that bust of Socrates.

For the occasion the Chronicler fished out of his robe an extraordinary device. Two pieces of glass had been fitted into a wooden frame, the ends of which were pierced for leathery thongs that ended in loops. Only when the old man fitted them to his eyes and slipped the loops over his ears did Ellery realize that they were hand-crafted spectacles. He seemed to have greater difficulty seeing through them than without them, so obviously the lenses had been salvaged from some mysterious out-world source and fitted into homemade frames. Perhaps they went with the office.

"Do I have your meaning, Elroï?" the Chronicler asked in a cracked tremolo. "Whence you come, the years have numbers, not names?"

"Yes."

"Thunderation! And do the people (*smick!*) have numbers as well?"

"No, names, unless they misbehave. Yes, this is our year 1944."

"(*Smick!*) 1944 *what*, Elroï?"

"A.D. That stands for *Anno Domini*. In the Year of Our Lord. Of the Christian era."

"Ne-e-e-ever (*smick!*) heard-of-it."

"Which year is it, Chronicler, according to the Quenan calendar?"

The Chronicler had been peering into a scroll taken at Ellery's request from its repository jar in his record room. He looked up from the scroll at Ellery's question, amazed.

"The year it is *now*? (*Smick!*) Blessed be the Wor'd! How should I know?"

Half amused, half confused, "Who, then, should know?" Ellery asked.

"Why, no one! No one at all! (*Smick!*) A year's got no name till it's over, you know. How could it? The Crownsil meets on Lastday and decides which name to give it. The year that has just gone past was recently named The Year the Black Ewe Had Twins. Before that there was The Year of the Big Plums. Then The Year of the Caterpillars. Then The Year of the Great Wind. Then . . ."

Ellery followed him back, back, back . . . through The Year of the Lost Harvest, The Year the Earth Shook, The Year of the Great Rains, The Year the Teacher Took Barzill to Wife, and so on; until, finally, The Year of the Eastern Pilgrimage, when the Quenanites had made their exodus from San Francisco. Which, indeed, had been 1873.

"So you see (*smick!*), we have been in our Valley years to the number . . . seventy, yes! (*smick!*) seventy. That's how many years I have counted for you. And the number may be confirmed by the old writings."

The Chronicler gestured toward the scroll. The writing was in the same strange "Chancery hand" Ellery had seen the Successor employ in the scriptorium. Was it possible that some Teacher or Successor in a long-gone generation had been employed by a London law firm—perhaps even before the days when Dickens was reporting parliamentary debates?

Possible? In this place, Ellery thought, anything was possible.

"The old writings," Ellery murmured. "Do they record anything, Chronicler, about the fifty silver dollars?"

Up jumped the Chronicler, stuffing the scroll into its jar and replacing the cover. "They do, they do!" He trotted back, replaced the jar on its shelf, took down another jar, and trotted back with it. "Let me see (*smick!*) 'Year of the Last Pilgrimage'—yes, hmm, hmm." He ran his finger down a column, failed to find what he sought, rolled the scroll up on one side, unrolled it on another. "Hah! Look—"

There it was, in the same archaic writing, on the yellowed paper. *this year the crownsil debated what to do with the fifty silver dollars, which some suggested that, we possessing greater wealth than this which needs be counted, it be buried and forgotten. but instead the crownsil voted that it be deposited in the sanquetum, there to lie until such time as may be otherwise decided.*

The strange letters danced before his eyes. Ellery drooped. He was exhausted again. What was the matter with him? He struggled with his thoughts.

Fifty . . . He had failed to count the coins in the two columns. But surely they hadn't been as many as fifty?

"What happened to the rest of the silver dollars, Chronicler?"

The old official looked puzzled. "Rest of them (*smick!*)? Nay, Guest, I know nothing of that. Only the Teacher—blessed be the Wor'd for his continuing presence amongst us—is permitted to enter the forbidden room. The dollars are kept there, with the holy book."

"Yes, the holy book. What does its title mean?"

"The Book of Mk'n?"

"Mk'n? I thought the Teacher called it Mk'h?"

The Chronicler frowned at his own error. "According to the old writings—and all is written with the pen of remembrance—the lost book was thought to be the Book of Mk'n. That is, by those who held that there *was* such a book. Others (*smick!*) have held that there was not.

But so the Teacher called it, and his father before him —Mk'n. Then, five years ago, in The Year of Many Birds, the Teacher found the lost book; and after he had studied the old writings again, he believed that we had always misread or miswritten the title—that it was Mk'h and not Mk'n. And since then we have called it the Book of Mk'h. For all is as the Teacher says."

"But what does the title *mean?*"

The old man shrugged. "Who knows? Do names always have a meaning?"

After a while Ellery left and sought out the Teacher. He asked if he might borrow a donkey and take a brief leave of the Valley.

"You will be back," the patriarch said. It was neither a question or a request.

"Of course."

"Then go, Elroï, and the Wor'd go with you."

Ellery had not been certain of his motives in fixing on a Quenanite beast for his journey instead of taking his car, and the long, uncomfortable donkey ride did not make them quite clear. Finally he decided that he had been moved simply by a sense of fitness. In the land of the prophet one went mounted in the manner of the prophet. (And a rude manner it was: no proper saddle, only a worn felt pad; a frayed grass rope for bridle and bit; and a long reed in place of whip or quirt.)

He was also undecided whether Otto Schmidt, *Prop.*, was more surprised to see his customer of a few days before come "riding on the foal of an ass" than to see him again at all. At last the storekeeper's mouth closed and a delighted smile spread so widely across his moon-face that his smudge of mustache threatened to reach his ears.

"It's you!" he cried.

"Hello, Mr. Schmidt," Ellery said, dismounting. "Where can I tether Lightning?"

The stout little man bustled forward. "Here, here in the shade. Let me get him a bucket of water and some bread. Oh, you brought feed. Here, let me fix it for him.

Well! Mr. Quinn, was it? Or Kean? My goodness, where you been? And how come you're riding this here old jackass? What happened to your car . . . ?"

Ellery walked into the store, inhaling the cool, damp aroma of ancient wood and cinnamon and coffee and vinegar and cloves and kerosene. Everything was as he had last seen it: the spirals of flypaper, the faded colorphoto of Franklin D. Roosevelt, the worn counter with its brass measure set into the top (and how long ago was it, Ellery wondered, that calico or canvas or gingham or unbleached muslin had been measured off on it?), the antique soda-pop cooler . . .

He sat down at one of the tables and immediately winced. An occasional canter on the Central Park bridle path had not been really adequate training for a three-hour ride through the desert on the back of a vigorous male donkey.

"Well, by golly!" Mr. Schmidt had scurried in, beaming. "You found the road like I told you? You get to Vegas? Say! Is that why you're on the jack? I bet you lost your car playing crap. Or was it in the slot machines? Or—it's none of my business, of course."

Ellery smiled noncommittally. "Any chance of getting something to eat, Mr. Schmidt? Or I'll have to eat Lightning."

"Surest thing you know! You're in luck! Bill Hone, you wouldn't know him, makes a special side trip through here once a week on his way from Hamlin to Vegas. I give him my ration stamps and he picks the meat up for me. Well! Bill was by this morning and he left me some of the nicest steak I've seen since I was cutting meat back in the old home town. How about a T-bone and maybe a couple of eggs? And there's some boiled potatoes I could country-fry, and I baked up a batch of peach tarts . . ." He ran down, evidently searching his mind for additions to the menu.

Ellery swallowed the water in his mouth.

"Oh, yes," he said. "Starting with some coffee?" And added, "Will you join me?"

"Well, by golly!" said Otto Schmidt. "I will . . . !"

The coffee was fresh and strong; the steaks had been pan-broiled over a slow fire. Ellery found his sense of purpose slipping away in the pleasure of once more eating civilized food. How long ago had it been? There was no time in Quenan, and not much more awareness of its passage here in the End-of-the-World Store. With an effort he pulled his dawdling mind back to the business that had brought him.

"What can you tell me about the silver dollar the old fellow gave you last Sunday, Mr. Schmidt?"

Otto Schmidt paused, a crisp brown-edged chunk of potato halfway to his mouth, a drip of egg on his mustache. He stared. He blinked; his smile faded. Then the potato continued to its destination, and he chewed it slowly.

"So. You met up with those two hermits. Well, they're kind of queer, but live and let live is my motto. They don't bother no one and I hope no one bothers them—"

"Mr. Schmidt," Ellery said gently. "Otto. No one's going to bother them. Or you. I simply want to know about that silver dollar I saw him give you."

The corpulent little storekeeper declared earnestly that there was no law against silver dollars. Gold, now, he said, that was different. In '35—no, '34—time went by so slow out here you lost track—a fellow came through in a touring car with rubber curtains buying old gold—

"Otto."

"—said his name was Haggemeyer, he'd been in Mexico with Black Jack Pershing chasing Pancho Villa. He'd set up his own business afterwards in Laredo but the depression wiped him out—"

"Otto . . ."

"—borrowed some money against his pension and was going around buying up old gold. He showed me his license—had to have a license for gold—"

"*Otto!*"

The storekeeper stopped, looking apprehensive.

"Otto, nobody's accusing you of breaking the law. Here, take a look at these."

Ellery produced his wallet. As police card followed police card, Otto Schmidt's eyes opened wider and wider. At the sight of the two letters from Washington, they bulged.

"Sayyy! You must be a pretty important fellow." His eyes shone as he leaned over the table. "Does this have anything to do with the war effort?"

Ellery recast the question. "Do I have anything to do with the war effort?" And answered it, quite truthfully, "Yes, I have."

Otto leaned back, unmistakably awed. With one final *"Well!"* and a muttered, "That's okay, then," he got up and went over to his safe—a safe as short and squat as he was, with the flaked remains of an American flag and eagle still faintly visible in faded red, white, blue, and yellow on its door. He came back with a battered old ledger.

"You got to understand the situation when I bought this place," he said with false-hearty defensiveness. "I don't know how long this old hermit had been dealing with the former owner, but they didn't trade for cash money; no, sir. The hermit and his wagon would come around every now and then with produce—hides, wool, flaxseed oil, honey, beeswax—truck like that; and the fellow who had the store would give him credit.

"Then came the depression. Then came me. But the depression was still on, and in a little while I found out that my suppliers, my wholesalers, wouldn't take produce any more—not in such small quantities anyway. Cash on the barrelhead, they said. Credit? 'Credit is dead,' I told the old hermit. 'No more produce. Has to be cash.' 'What's that?' he asked me. Well, I put my hand in my pocket and I had a lone silver dollar and I pulled it out and showed it to him. That old man looked at the silver dollar, then he looked at me like I'd shown him a dirty picture. And out he goes without saying a word.

"Next time he showed up was November, 1930. Here it is, written down, see? *November 12, 1930. Hermit. Carson City silver dollar, 1873.* I didn't know much about old coins, still don't, but I figured it's got to be worth a lot more than just one hundred cents, and I told him so. I was due to make a visit to L.A., and I offered to take his coin with me and see what I could get for it. He agreed, though I could see he was kind of struggling with himself."

Otto had taken the silver dollar around to various dealers in downtown Los Angeles, and he had finally sold it for the highest price offered in 1930—$90. When the old man of the hills returned to the End-of-the-World Store, they made a deal: the proprietor would retain $18 for his trouble and the old hermit would be credited with $72 against his account.

The old man visited the store once or twice a year, and Otto noted each transaction in the ledger. Sometimes the hermit would bring one of the *CC* 1873 dollars with him, sometimes not, depending on the state of his account. When one of the coins passed hands, Otto held onto it until his next trip to Los Angeles, where he would shop around for the best price, sell the coin, keep 20 percent commission for himself (to Ellery's amusement, the figure was between a literary agent's commission and an art dealer's), and credit the balance to the hermit's account.

"And that's the way it's been for thirteen and a half years," the little storekeeper said. "The old bird seems to have a whole supply of 'em—I figured he must be some kind of prospector from way back who went a little nutty from too much sun, and the younger fellow's his grandson or something."

"How many *CC dollars* has he turned over to you since the first time?"

"Including last Sunday? Well, I got to figure . . ." Figure Otto did, with moistened finger riffling and rumbling the pages, while Ellery fidgeted. Finally the storekeeper announced, "Nineteen, all told."

Ellery's first thought was that there was something

wrong about the number. The thought kept niggling, but he could not come to terms with it. Impatiently he asked Schmidt what kind of things the old man bought on his visits.

"Oh, rock salt, kerosene, nails, stuff like that. No, never candy or wine or anything fancy. Seed? Not that I remember. But lots of paper. Must do a heap of writing. And, oh, yes! he once bought a piece of furniture."

"Furniture!"

Otto Schmidt nodded. "Sure was funny, what happened that day—the book and all. I can remember, Mr. Green—Breen—?"

"Queen," Ellery said. "Let's not wander afield, Otto. You mentioned a piece of furniture and a book. What about them? And when was this?"

The storekeeper referred to his ledger. It had occurred on April 8, 1939—"the year the war broke out in Europe." The hermit had come in . . . alone? Yes, Mr. Queen, alone. "Never laid eyes on the younger fellow till last year. Well, the old man left a silver dollar, picked up his supplies, and was getting ready to go. The book was on the counter and he spotted it. Something real strange seemed to happen to him. You've noticed his eyes? They're kind of . . . on fire all the time. Well, this time they blazed up like Fourth of July. And he went into a trance, like, shook and mumbled, seemed to be having some sort of a fit, and—well, *praying,* like, all at the same time.

"When he calmed down, he asked me how much credit it would take to buy the book, how many silver dollars."

"What book was it?" Ellery asked, failing to keep the eagerness out of his voice.

"Oh, some book sent to me from Europe; I have relatives on the other side. I'd tried to read it, but it didn't hold my interest, so I put it away. I'd come across it again and was having another try at it when the hermit came in."

"But what was the title of the book?"

"To tell you the truth, Mr. Queen, I can't recall. Anyway, when he said he wanted to buy it, and I said no—"

"You said no? Why, when it didn't interest you?"

"I don't know," said Otto Schmidt. "It just didn't seem right—I mean, selling a present from a relative. But he kept after me to let him buy it. The more I said no, the more he said yes. Got all hotted up, the old man did —offered me all the silver dollars he had. In the end I said he could have it—as a gift. You know, he blessed me? And then he pointed to an old walnut china closet I used as a showcase for notions and such, and he offered to buy *that*. I charged him five dollars for it."

"Didn't he say why he wanted the book?"

"No, just wrapped it up, very careful, loaded his wagon, and left. I guess if you're not touched in the head to begin with you don't become a hermit. You know, he couldn't even read the book? Admitted it when I asked him. But he just had to have it."

The question of the book was not going to be solved here in the store, obviously. Nor the question of the silver dollars. Their number . . . why was he so disturbed about their number?

Here is wisdom: let him who hath understanding count the number of the Beast, for it is the number of a man, and his number is six hundred sixty and six . . . Interesting that this verse from the Apocalypse of John should enter his mind just now. But of course 666 was far too large. He had to know what the number was—he simply had to. To do that he must return and count the coins in the holy arque.

Now!

The nearer Ellery got to Crucible Hill, the moodier he felt. It was with an effort that he had restrained himself from trying to beat the donkey into a gallop. A heavy depression had settled on him; a black, bleak melancholy. The wearisome journey on the beast, his mood and malaise, gloomily recalled the state of mind and body that had brought his work in Hollywood to such an abrupt halt; and he asked himself if he had ever really recovered. And he asked himself if he ever would.

He looked up at the sky, observing with surprise that it was rapidly darkening, although it was not yet sunset.

Was a storm brewing? Perhaps a falling barometer was causing his depression.

By the time he had reached the crest of Crucible Hill, the sky was almost black and the Valley was in profound shadow. He could discern nothing clearly. Even his ears seemed affected; he could hear none of the usual sounds of Quenan. Jogging slowly down the inner slope, eyes open but not seeing, he was almost upon the Holy Congregation House before he looked up, and was shocked.

Gathered before the building was a crowd which must have represented almost the entire population of the Valley.

And all were silent.

And it was like night.

The blackened air had a green tinge to it, and through this unnatural light the yellow lampshine from inside the House fell through the open doorway with ghastly effect, like a scene from hell. The stunned folk of Quenan stood rooted as though by some paralyzing force, some terrible horror they groped vainly to apprehend.

Ellery's heart swelled, then constricted as if squeezed by a giant hand. *The Teacher!* Was it his own death the old man had sensed approaching?

Dismounting hastily, Ellery ran through the crowd and into the House. And there indeed was the Teacher —but not dead, only looking like death; looking for the first time every year of his great age. And at his feet lay a man.

Storical.

The Storesman was dead. But no assault by nature on heart or brain had stormed his life and taken it. The sun-dark forehead had been crumpled by a barbarous blow: bones had shattered, blood had spurted, so that head and face were thickly redly wet with it, as if a bucket of paint had been flung at him. And head and neck and shoulders lay in a pool of it, still glistening.

Numbly, Ellery sought its cause; and there it was, lying on the floor of the Holy Congregation House a little to one side of the Storesman's body, an instrument he had—somehow—expected to find: a heavy hammer, spattered with scarlet.

"The "great trouble," then, had come at last to the Valley of Quenan. There was no longer need to wonder in what form it would make its dread appearance.

It was the kind of trouble for which Ellery had been predestined; and his brain cleared, and he sprang forward.

At the back of the Storesman's head there was another wound; but Ellery's practiced fingers told him that it was not, by itself, a mortal blow. The smashing hammer on the forehead had taken Storicai's life. He parted the curly hair; and among the curls he spied—first one, then another, then still another—tiny particles of what looked like plaster.

Ellery frowned. Nowhere in Quenan had he seen plaster. He examined the speck again, this time with his lens.

They were clay—bits of hardened clay.

Gently he opened the clenched hand of the dead man. The Storesman had died clutching a button, a metal button, its sundered threads still attached; and on the button's face there was a crude and curious symbol.

Ellery did not pause to examine it. He dropped the button into a glassine envelope from the leather kit he had had a messenger fetch from his luggage.

Strapped to the left wrist of the dead man was Ellery's watch. He lifted the wrist, the hand dangling. Ellery looked up. "He was so taken with this watch—"

Before Ellery's eyes, beyond surprises now, the Teacher drew himself up to his full height, shedding his mantle of years swiftly; and his voice, when it came, was rich and strong again. "We must not say"—he gestured toward the watch, glittering gold in the dimly golden light—"we must not say, Elroï, 'It would have been better had he never seen it.' "

But this was no time for riddles; and Ellery returned his attention to the watch. The crystal was savagely smashed, the dial deeply dented; no mere fall would have caused this havoc. No, Storicai had thrown up his left hand in an attempt to ward off one of the hammer blows, and he did, catching the blow on the watch; but he failed to stop the next blow, and staggering, grappling, clutching, grasping the button, he had fallen dead.

The hands had stopped at 4:20.

The time was now (he had it checked) 4:58. Ellery had been here about three minutes.

Systematically he went through the dead man's clothing. And in an inner pocket he found what he had altogether forgotten—a crude duplicate of the key to the sanquetum.

So the thief in the night had been Storicai. Or . . . had it been?

Ellery sighed. Even in Eden.

He straightened up, pointing to the hammer. The old man's face was now remarkably calm, although his eyes —those prophet's eyes—were sadder than Ellery had yet seen them. But they kindled Ellery's gesture.

"Thus it was," the Teacher began. "One of the legs of the Crownsil table on this side had loosened, and I was intending to ask the Successor to mend it after his studies and writing. I deemed it not important enough to call to the attention of the Carpentersmith, but lacked time to do it myself.

"Therefore I placed the hammer from my tool chest in the center of this table as a reminder to me to ask the Successor to repair the table leg."

Ellery wrapped the hammer carefully in one of his large handkerchiefs. While he was so occupied, the Successor came running in through the still-open door (and still the still crowd stood outside), calling, "I have searched everywhere, Master—"

"He is here," the Teacher said, indicating Ellery.

The young man gasped for breath, looking at the body on the floor. He shuddered and gave a short cry.

"You may go to your room," said the old man gently.

"Oh, but please." Ellery stopped the Successor. "Will you first go to the scriptorium and bring me fifteen pieces of paper?"

Even in Eden the same things had to be done.

Through the doorway a light breeze blew, bringing Ellery the memory of the first hint he had had, then unrecognized, of the existence of Quenan, the smell of burning sagebrush. The same breeze set the room's single lamp to swinging, as the lamp in the sanquetum had swung only that morning. But now the shadows seemed large with doom.

He said to the Teacher, "Please summon the Crownsil and the Superintendent. There is something I must ask them to do."

The summons took only the speaking, for those he named were in the throng outside. The members entered and took their accustomed places; even the very old Slave, who had been ill, it appeared, and had to be carried in; then, at Ellery's gesture, the door was closed. It seemed to him that he could hear another sigh (or was it a moan?), but this might have been imagination.

Once again great waves of stupefying fatigue, so familiar now, began to break against him. He shook them off like a dog.

On the Crownsil table, for the first time since the trial of Belyar the Weaver, were set things appertaining to crime. Then there had been nothing but bolts of cloth and the stolen pieces cut therefrom. Now Ellery laid down his leather kit. It contained the accessories of his other trade—fingerprint outfit, springback measuring tape, compass, flashlight, scissors, tweezers, small jars, rubber gloves, plastic tape, glassine envelopes, notebook, pencil, a marking pen, labels, a .38 Police Positive, a box of shells.

There had been times when he had had to call on all the contents of the kit; but on this occasion Ellery took from it only the fingerprinting equipment and the marking pen.

"What is it, Elroï," asked the Teacher, not flinching at sight of the strange objects, although most of the kit's contents were as mysterious to him as to the shrinking Crownsil, "what is it that you wish of us?"

"Teacher," Ellery replied softly, "I wish to go among you and record on these pieces of paper the imprint of your fingertips—the fingertips of all present. It is a simple thing, and there is no pain attached to it. Each of you will touch no paper but the single paper I set before you—is that clear?"

"The thing is clear, Elroï, its meaning is not," said the old man. "Nevertheless, it shall be as you say. I observe that you called for fifteen pieces of paper, although—excluding you—there are only fourteen of us. Is it your wish to record the imprint of the fingertips of him who has ceased, also?"

Ellery's head snapped back in surprise at the old man's shrewdness. "Storicai's? Yes, Teacher. I shall record his first."

And this he did, under their awed eyes, to the accompaniment of their quickened breathing. When he rose to face them with his paraphernalia, their breathing ceased altogether for a moment. But their venerable leader, observing their dread, stepped forward and said in a steady voice, "Among the living, Elroï, I shall be the first," and he held out his corded, blackened hands.

So Ellery took the fingerprints of the Teacher, and of the Successor, and of the Superintendent, and of the eleven surviving members of the Crownsil of the Twelve; and on each paper, under the fingerprints, he marked the name of the office held by the official whose fingertips had deposited the impressions.

"And now, Quenan?"

"Now we may be alone, Teacher."

"Do you wish him who has ceased to remain?"

"No, he may now be removed."

The patriarch nodded. "Crownsil and Superintendent," he addressed the officials of his people, "do you leave the holy house now, taking him who has ceased with you to be prepared for the place of peace. Tell the people to return to their homes or their tasks; while we live, the duties of life must go on. Successor, you may retire to your chambers. Blessed be the Wor'd, in grief as in joy." He raised his hand in benediction and dismissal.

And while some were reverently removing the body of the Storesman, and others carried the Slave away, and the rest were trooping out in silence, Ellery thought: And now I've committed a crime, too . . . For in whichever state the Valley existed—he had never thought to ask Otto Schmidt!—there was a law-enforcement agency, at least a county sheriff, whom he should be notifying that a murder had been committed. Yet until this moment, watching the Quenanites carting off the body of the murder victim to be prepared for burial, the thought had not crossed his mind.

Well, he could not. What an enormously greater crime it would be to open the doors of the Valley of Quenan to the world as it was!

When the last of the Crownsil had left, and the door was shut again, Ellery said, "Teacher, when we first met you told me that my coming was foretold, that I was to be your guide through a time of great trouble that was to come upon you."

The old man bowed deeply in assent, then raised his head so that once more it was partly hidden by his hood.

"Then you must tell me everything that happened this afternoon, and you must tell me the time that everything happened, as exactly as you know."

The ancient lids slipped down, leaving only slits. Then each eye was wide open, seeing across time.

"So," the prophet said. "At noon I returned from the fields and meditated in my room for the hour of the midday meal, of which I no longer partake. I knew that it was noon, for so the shadow—by its absence—told me. At one o'clock I went to the schoolhouse. I sensed it to be one o'clock—after all these years my body had become a timepiece of itself. And I taught the children for the space of one hour. In the schoolhouse stands a clock, and when it said two o'clock (and when I knew it to be that time) I returned here, to the Holy Congregation House.

"I should have found the Successor at his studies. Instead he was lingering in the doorway hoping to see a certain young woman go by, I am sure. Passion is natural, even holy; but it has its time and place, and these were not the proper ones. I therefore sent him to the scriptorium, and to remove temptation I locked him in and retained the key. Then someone came with a message that the Slave was ill and wished to see me—"

"About the Slave, later," Ellery said gravely. "First I wish to visit the scriptorium again. Will you come with me, Teacher?"

The Successor was not in the scriptorium; apparently he had retired to his sleeping chamber next door. On his original visit to the scribe's tiny workroom, Ellery had been in no condition to observe details. Now he saw that it contained two little writing desks, two small benches, and shelves crowded with scrolls and scroll jars, piles of paper, reels of thread, bundles of quills and reed pens, jugs of ink, and other items of the scrivener's profession.

By the side of each desk stood a tall candelabrum whose sconces held heavy brown beeswax candles.

In the two walls of the scriptorium that faced the outdoors were the same type of tall slit-windows he had seen in the Teacher's room—far too narrow for the passage of even a small child. Once locked in, then, the Successor would have had either to wait until the Teacher returned to unlock the door of the scriptorium or to break down the door himself. The door showed no sign that it had been forced.

Ellery and the old man left the scriptorium as they had entered and visited it, in silence.

"Would you go on now, Teacher?" Ellery asked.

The old man continued his narrative. He had returned to his schoolroom, performed his duties there until the hour of three, and then gone back to the Holy Congregation House. Whereupon he had remembered the message about the Slave and his illness. Before he left, he recalled the weak leg of the table and placed the hammer on it—in the center—as a reminder to himself later to ask the Successor to make the repairs.

Then the prophet had set out for the Slave's house.

Before the Slave's house stood a sundial. The Teacher estimated that the time was about 3:15 when he passed it.

"I remained with him for an hour. I would have stayed longer; we were young men together. And I returned"—he was speaking with the most deliberate care —"and I returned, then, at a time very close to a quarter past the hour of four. I . . . returned . . ."

What was the old man trying to say?

"At four-twenty," Ellery said gently, "Storicai was dead."

The Teacher made a great effort. "Yes, the Storesman was . . . dead. He was lying, even as you saw him, in his blood on the floor of the meeting room here."

"This is difficult for you," Ellery murmured. "But you must go on, Teacher."

"I unlocked the door of the scriptorium, released the Successor, and sent him at once to seek you out, if you had yet returned from your journey. For it had come at last—the great trouble had come down upon the tribe of Quenan; and I knew a need for him who is called Elroï, and again Quenan. For all was as it had been written."

Ellery sighed. Theology, prophecy, soothsaying—it was not through these that the riddle of Storicai's murder would be solved . . . Storicai, who had been so enchanted by the glitter of the wrist watch, the first wrist watch he had ever seen, who had been so childishly pleased at being allowed to wear it. And who had worn it all the rest of his life . . . "Did you ask the Successor if he had overheard anything—an unusual sound, voices—while he was locked in the scriptorium?"

The furrow between the brow tufts deepened. "Nay, Quenan. Let us ask him now."

But the Successor, his angel's face still white above its boyish beard, could gasp only, "I heard nothing, nothing!"

With another sigh, Ellery asked the Teacher to retire to his room also. But first he obtained the key to the sanquetum.

His hand on the doorknob, he hesitated as before, feeling again that if he entered the forbidden room he would defile it. But there was no turning aside now. He slipped the key into the lock and found, to his amazement, that the door was not locked at all. Quickly Ellery slipped inside the sanquetum and shut the door behind him.

The eternal lamp hung from an old brass chain. The chain ran through a metal eye sunk into the center of the ceiling and over to a hook fixed in one of the walls, to which it was secured through one of its links. There were enough links to leave several feet of chain dangling from the hook. Ellery nodded; it was a practical if primitive device, for after all it was easier to slip the chain off the hook in the wall and lower the lamp for refilling than to have to climb a ladder.

He unhooked the chain and let out the slack so that the lamp just cleared his head. The dark circle on the floor where the lamp's shadow fell expanded, but the rest of the chamber became lighter. Ellery hooked the chain so that the lamp would be fixed in the lower position; and down on all fours he went.

He scanned the flooring square inch by square inch, making grotesquely shifting shadows on the walls.

He made his first discovery under the arque—a shard of clay with a purple-glazed outer surface.

Ellery rose, looking keenly about. The huge scroll jar on his right seemed to be sitting poorly on its wooden base, canted a little as if hastily moved or set there. Yet he was sure the big urn had occupied the base properly during his morning survey of the sanquetum.

He turned his attention to the arque. The glass of the china closet was unbroken; but on a corner of the walnut frame, level with the bottom shelf, he made out a faint gleam . . . a stain, darkish sticky . . . for he touched it, and some of it came away on his finger. Blood. Blood that had not been there in the morning.

And the coins?

The two columns of silver dollars which he had left so neatly stacked in the morning, were no longer so. Each column leaned a little, and in one column a milled edge protruded.

Standing before the arque, in the flickering light, Ellery reconstructed the events of the afternoon. Clearly, it was Storicai who had secretly made the duplicate key for the sanquetum door—Storicai who, while the Teacher was visiting the sick old Slave and while the Successor was locked in the scriptorium, had once more committed the sin of entering the Holy Congregation House without leave; Storicai, who had committed the far greater sin of entering the forbidden room for the purpose of stealing the silver treasure of the community.

Forbidden entry, sacrilege, a thieving heart—who would have dreamed the simple Storesman capable of these?

And even as the greedy man had crouched in the sanquetum, perhaps, in the very act of laying impious hands on the coins, he had been attacked from behind. Someone had rushed into the holy room, seized the right-hand prayer jar, raised it high, and brought it down on the back of the Storesman's head. The jar must have shattered or, at the least, broken partly—witness the overlooked shard under the arque and the bits of clay in the dead man's hair; but this blow had not been the killing blow. The Storesman had fallen, unconscious or dazed; in falling, he had struck his head on the corner of the arque, and had stained it with his blood.

And all this in the holy of holies, in the presence of the scrolls enjoining peace and the love of brothers. Joab at the horns of the altar; à Beckett in the cathedral.

The striker of the blow must have turned and fled. And the Storesman, recovering quickly, ran after the witness to his crimes and caught up with him in the meeting room. And here they must have struggled (in panting silence, or else the Successor from behind his locked door would have heard the struggle); and Storicai must have tried to kill his assailant of the sanquetum to preserve his guilty secret—for by the law of Quenan theft was a capital crime—and the witness, cornered by the Crownsil table, would have had to fight for his life. The hammer being on the table where the Teacher had left it, the witness had snatched it up and struck the Storesman with it at least twice: once on the upflung wrist, shattering the crystal, denting the dial, and stopping the mechanism of the watch; and a second and lethal time, on the forehead.

Who was the witness to Storicai's crimes and the perpetrator of the first man-slaying in the history of the Valley?

Ellery again became aware of the curious something about the coins that had been gnawing at him all day. What was it?

Their *number*—that was it! In his account of the colony's wanderings, the Teacher had said that his father had brought to the Valley silver dollars to the number of fifty; and the Chronicler had confirmed this from his records. Fifty; and according to Schmidt's ledger, the Teacher had expended nineteen of them at the End-of-the-World Store.

Leaving thirty-one.

Ellery stared at the two columns of coins in the china closet. Each pillar was of the same height. Meaning that each contained the same number of silver dollars— meaning that, whatever the total number of coins, it had to be an *even* number . . . Of course! There could not be thirty-one!

This was what had been nagging him since his visit to Schmidt's store. The number thirty-one disturbed the perfect symmetry of everything in the forbidden room; it had started some subliminal computer clicking in Ellery's head.

How account for both columns containing the same number of coins when one of the columns should be taller than the other by the thickness of a single silver dollar? Was a silver dollar missing?

Then Ellery remembered. It was not missing; it had been expended in the time of Belyar the Weaver, when the Teacher had decreed exile for the cloth stealer instead of death. The man had been driven into the desert with sustenance for two days *and a single silver dollar*.

One from thirty-one gave an even number and explained the two columns of identical height.

And so Ellery reached into the arque and took out one of the pillars of coins, and counted its 1873 Carson City dollars, and he counted fifteen; and he replaced the column perfectly, and took out the other, and in this pillar he counted fifteen coins also.

It was just after he had put the second column carefully back beside its companion that he found himself holding on to the china closet with a roaring in his ears.

The Storesman had betrayed his Teacher, his faith, and his brothers of Quenan for thirty pieces of silver.

As the moment passed, Ellery came gradually to see that at the focus of his downcast eyes, on the arque's lower shelf, lay the book. It was still there, in the same place still, still open; evidently untouched since the morning.

His eyes felt as though they had been ground in sand. At first the lines of black-letter type on the open pages persisted in shifting about in a sort of tormented mock dance. But then they stiffened and stood still; and out of nowhere came the unspeakable thought . . . unspeakable.

It was a dream within a dream, and evilly dark through and through; even this, this movement of his hand—not willed, a nightmare gesture—reaching into the china closet and raising and turning the left-hand part of the open book so that he might see the front cover, and the spine.

And he saw.

And what he saw he glared at like an idiot aroused for one lucid moment.

The mind rejected it. Unacceptable! it cried. Except in a dream. Even in a dream.

And it was no dream. It was true.

And it was too much.

It was a long time before Ellery recovered sufficiently to withdrew his hand; and then he spent another interval, timeless, staring at the hand.

The holy book. The Book of Mk'h, the Teacher had called it.

Yes, there they were, the letters on the cover that had so fired the old man when he laid eyes on the book lying on Schmidt's counter . . . that had led the patriarch to offer anything, even his entire store of silver coins, for its possession.

The "lost" book of Quenan, the Teacher had called it.

Ellery did not remember leaving the sanquetum, locking its door behind him, walking through the meeting room; he did not remember hearing the uneven echoes of his footsteps.

He remembered only standing in the open and gulping great gulps of air as if he could never gulp enough.

V

THURSDAY

April 6.

THE HAGS PURSUED him through the night; leered, gibbered, squatted on his chest mocking his pleas for breath. He knew that it was a dream, that he had only to open his eyes. But the effort was too great. He groaned, he babbled, he moaned; and so, moaning, he woke up at last.

He was chilled, numb, bone-tired; the haunted hours of sleep had brought him no surcease. Muttering, he groped for the blanket and turned over with a heave of desperation . . . In the corners of the room the hags were gathered, whispering. He strained to hear what they were saying, peered through the darkness. That was how he discovered his mistake—they were not the hags at all; he had been deceived by the robes: they were the members of the Crownsil, speaking together in disquieted voices, glancing dubiously at the piece of paper each held in his hand.

Now they were passing the papers from hand to hand *to handsome gathering groaning grinding troubled old troubling old man old mandaring mandrake mandragora*

99

*agora a gore gore agr grrr and so growling and gathering
up the gathering gathering*

Give me those! Ellery cried. You'll spoil the fingerprints!

—He shut his eyes, and by this he knew that they had
just been open and that he had cried out aloud. He
opened his eyes again. He was standing by the window
grinding his teeth. Outside ran gray morning. He was
shivering and his body was one great ache. And he remembered what had happened yesterday, and what
must happen today.

The misery of man is great upon him . . .

He dressed and carried his toilet kit to the rear of the
communal kitchen for hot water and he washed and
shaved and stumbled into the dining room. The first
shift of the people were at breakfast, a few speaking in
low tones, most speaking not at all. At Ellery's entrance
all speech stopped.

Some looked at him shyly; others with awe—the unfamiliar man and the unfamiliar crime; must they not be
connected, to be dreaded equally? Others regarded him
with faces full of adoration: had not the Teacher said
that the Guest's coming was foretold? And still others
showed him unchanged countenances, accepting and respectful.

But no one ventured to talk to him.

Ellery ate and drank what was set before him, con-
scious mainly that it was hot and filling.

He returned to his room to dispose of his toilet kit
and consider his course.

For a time he wrote in his notebook.

Then he put it away and went out to do what had to
be done.

Ellery could hardly remember the time when he had
not been struck by the recurrence of the great and fa-
mous across the shifting planes of space-time. In his
boyhood, he recalled, it had been Roman statuary coming to life. Mr. Tobias, who taught him civics, might

have been the fraternal twin of Scipio Africanus. Father
O'Toole, of the Roman Catholic church around the corner, might have stepped out of Nero's toga only the
night before. Patrolman Isador Rosen, Inspector
Queen's partner when both were pounding a beat, was a
dead ringer for Julius Caesar.

And so it went, in cycles, or perhaps Ellery was only
cyclically aware of it: Queen Victoria would sell him a
ticket to the movie; Whistler's Mother sat opposite him
on the bus; Beethoven delivered the laundry; Ivan the
Terrible leaned over the bar and asked, "Wottle it be?";
Robert E. Lee offered to draw his picture for a dollar
on a Greenwich Village sidewalk.

Such a cycle was evidently in motion now. Winston
Churchill had placed the porridge (if it was porridge)
before him at breakfast. Marie Dressler had removed
the empty bowl. And here was Bernard Shaw, with
dried slip on his beard, explaining how he made pottery.
It gave Ellery the queerest feeling as he stared at the
wheels and the kilns and watched the author of *Mrs.
Warren's Profession* strew a handful of salt inside one of
the kilns to give the tiles that were firing there a simple
glaze.

Ellery took the shard he had found in the sanquetum
from his pocket. "You don't use salt to produce this
purple glaze, do you?"

"Oh, no," said non-Shaw, the Potter. "Different
process altogether. For prayer jars, I mean."

"Then this came from a prayer jar?"

The Potter nodded. The smile that had graced his
bearded face while he was discussing his work died.

"Yesterday a prayer jar was broken. The prayer jars
are holy, for they contain the things of the Wor'd and
they stand in the sanquetum, the forbidden room in the
Holy Congregation House. The last time one was broken was the day the earth shook. There are never more
than four—the two in the sanquetum, and two spare
ones that are kept packed in wool and straw to protect
them. They are not easily made, nor often . . . Yesterday

one broke. For others the earth did not shake, perhaps. But it shook for me when I heard and saw, and it has not stopped shaking."

The Potter's workshop was stifling in the heat from the kiln. How must it feel to meet murder for the first time? "The broken jar has been deplaced in the sanquetum, then?"

"Yes." Someone broke into song not far off, and stopped abruptly after the first few notes. As if suddenly reminded, or suddenly remembering. "The Teacher came and asked me for a new one."

"Did he tell you why?"

The tufted white brows drew together, and the deep voice deepened. "He told me that the time of great trouble had come. I wondered, for I had seen no sign. And he asked for another prayer jar. So I understood that the shattering of the one to be replaced must be the sign. Not until later, when there was great running about and crying out, did I learn that Storicai the Storesman had himself been shattered. For is not each man," he sighed, "also a vessel of the Wor'd?"

"When did he come, the Teacher, to ask for a replacement jar for the forbidden room?" Ellery managed to ask.

"Yesterday. In the afternoon."

Like all his people, the Potter did not think of time in exact terms. But there was a clock in the shop, an old wooden one with a pendulum and weights (used, the Potter explained, in calculating the work of the kilns), and there was his record of the Teacher's requisition. As near as they could, they settled the time of the Teacher's visit at 4:30.

Ten minutes after the murder.

As Ellery turned to leave, the Potter said, "I have known that the great trouble of which we have been told would come upon us in my lifetime, if I lived the full measure of my years."

Ellery stopped, surprised. "How did you know that, Potter?"

The man raised his hand, encrusted with slip—the

mixture of ground clay and water with which he worked —and pointed upward.

"Those machines that fly through the sky," he said. "For three years now they have come and gone in increasing numbers. Surely this is the sign of the great trouble that has befallen Quenan?"

"It is a sign of the great trouble that has befallen the world," Ellery said.

The Potter's beard rested on his broad chest. "Blessed be the Wor'd," he muttered. "In time of trouble, as in time of peace."

The stench of singed hoof, which he had not encountered since he was a boy, greeted Ellery at his next stop. So did the more recently familiar smell of fresh sawdust. Ulysses S. Grant was just finishing the job of shoeing a fat gray jenny.

"Blessed be the Wor'd," General Grant said. "I am the Carpentersmith." He slapped the she-ass on the rump, and she trotted away. *The ox knoweth his crib, and the ass his master's stall* . . .

Ellery returned the greeting, and for a moment no one said anything more. The apprentice folded up the bellows and went shyly about other tasks. The firebed dimmed slowly from orange-red to ashy gray. Grant reincarnate picked up a piece of wood—a wagon tongue or whippletree, Ellery guessed—and began carefully to pry off a piece of metal.

"Though my hands are busy," the man said, "my ears are not."

"Do you make the keys?"

The Carpentersmith paused to consider. Then, stooping to his work again, he said, "When keys are required I make them. But few are required because we have few locks. The feed bin must have a lock because some of our beasts are clever and otherwise would pry open the latches with their teeth and eat more than is good for them."

"What else is kept locked and so requires a key?"

They were not many. The small quantity of Valley-made black powder, kept on hand for blasting stumps and rocks (the Carpentersmith seemed to have no idea that the powder could be put to other uses), was locked against the children and animals. The store of charqui, or jerked beef (the wind- and sun-dried "jerky" of the Southwest), was also stored under lock and key against the occasional coyote that, emboldened by hunger in a poor hunting season, slunk into Quenan. And the house of the lackwit gnome who tended the cemetery had a lock—the only dwelling in the village so equipped—because of fears to which the little man could give no name: "But none wish to dispute with him, and whom does it harm?"

And, yes. Ah, yes.

The sanquetum.

The calloused hands still and it seemed to Ellery that the Carpentersmith's eyes formed tears.

The sanquetum. "When did you last make a key to the sanquetum?"

"I have never made one," the man mumbled.

"Then who—?"

"The sanquetum key in the Teacher's keeping was made by Smuel, who was Carpentersmith a very long time ago."

There was no help for it; he had to ask: "Could a key be made without your knowledge? Say, in the dead of night?"

The Carpentersmith straightened, and before he answered he deposited in a bin the strip of metal he had detached from the piece of wood.

"Guest," he said courteously, "I am not Carpentersmith by right, but by skill and preference. Anyone is free at any time to come here and work. Whether I am here or not; my work often takes me elsewhere in the Valley. You ask, 'Could a key be made without my knowledge?' And I answer, 'Why should it not be? Why must I know it?' "

Ellery sighed. This was another world, with another set of values. The primitive Polynesians were horrified that the masters of European ships should flog their sailors for, to them, the perfectly natural act of swimming ashore without leave to find women; yet they themselves matter-of-factly stole everything from the ships that was not tied down, and were bewildered at the savage resentment their thievery aroused.

"Let me put it this way," Ellery said patiently. "Did Storicai work in this shop recently? Could the Storesman have made a key?"

With equal patience the Carpentersmith said, "Guest, I have known Storicai all my life. He was often here, for he was Storesman. I was often at the storehouse, for I am Carpentersmith. For Storicai to be here was as common a sight as to see a bird roost in a tree. He could have made a hundred keys and I need not have known it.

"But"—Grant's broad shoulders sagged—"he will be here never more. All men must cease, blessed be the Wor'd; we come into the place left for us by others, we go from here that others may come after us. But no one in Quenan has ever ceased as Storicai ceased, and when I think of this I am sorely troubled, Guest, sorely."

Ellery produced a glassine envelope in which he was keeping the metal button he had pried from the dead Storesman's hand. "Have you seen this button before, Carpentersmith?"

"That is the Teacher's," the man said slowly. He hesitated. "Most use buttons of bone or wood. Those of us on the Crownsil, also the Successor and the Superintendent, wear buttons of horn. Only the Teacher wears buttons of metal." He pointed to the curious symbol on the button, and even as he did so Ellery recognized it as the capital letter *N*, done in the Quenanite script that so resembled the Chancery hand of a century before and six thousand miles' distance. "This *N*," said the Carpentersmith, "means *fifty*. It is a sacred number, and only the Teacher may use it." He hesitated again, and then he said timidly, "Guest, should you not return it to him?"

But Ellery was already out the door.

They were making wool blankets in the weaving shed, and the bitter, musty odor of the sheep hung like a fog. The Weaver paused at her loom, shifting a bit in her harness. She was a big woman, and of course, given a cigar, she could have passed anywhere for Amy Lowell.

Her voice was soft and rich. Yes, she did tailoring as well as weaving. Yes, the Teacher had come to her yesterday afternoon. He had said that a button was missing from his robe—not that he needed to tell her, she said, with a sad smile; she had observed it at once. She had sewn another one on then and there. She kept a supply of his metal buttons on hand at all times.

"What time was this, Weaver?" Ellery asked. He felt mean in the presence of this warmly glowing personality.

"Time?" She paused. "How curious that you should ask, Guest. I take little note of time. Weaving, sewing— you know, they are not like boiling milk. When my heart is light, the shuttle flies. When my heart is heavy —as it is now—the loom is heavy, too, and the work goes slowly.

"Yesterday, when the Teacher came, I was thinking little of time. For I was working on a new pattern—may I show it to you?"

The wool she had used was the color of the desert, and against this background she had woven, in black wool, a bird. Ellery squinted at it, trying to decide whether its subtle distortion was inherent in its design or a result of his tired eyes. Then, quite suddenly, he made it out. What had been woven was not the bird itself, but its shadow on the sandy ground. The illusion was startling.

"Did you do this?" he exclaimed, entranced.

"Do you like it," the woman murmured. "I am glad. Yes, it is my own. I am weaving this for my—for the Teacher's use."

The slip of the tongue told him that she was one of the old man's wives. For some reason, indefinable, the pulse in his neck thickened and began to throb.

"But the time," Ellery muttered. "You don't know what time it was?"

"I was not thinking of time," the rich voice said. "But the Teacher asked me. So I went and looked. I have a watch, an old gold one that was mine from my father, who had it from his. Inside this watch is written a thing which none of us here understands, not even the Teacher. It says, *'From the Men of the 17th. Vera Cruz, Cerro Gordo, Monterrey. 1848.'*"

Ellery closed his eyes. It seemed too much, somehow, this disgraceful echo of the past. "It refers," he said, choosing his words with care, "to an expedition made a generation before this colony was founded. Groups of men went to Mexico, a country to the south. I suppose that someone in your family—your father's grandfather, perhaps—must have been in charge of one of those groups, called the 17th. Afterward, the men of his group gave him the watch as a remembrance . . . The other words are the names of places in Mexico."

The Weaver nodded. "I am glad to know at last," she said, with shining eyes. "They must have loved him greatly to give him so rare a gift. Thank you for telling me. And now to answer your own question. The Teacher asked me the time. And by the watch the time was fifteen minutes before the hour of five."

"One more question, Weaver. Did the Teacher have a prayer jar with him?"

No. No, he did not. Once more her face saddened.

It was not till later that Ellery knew he had misunderstood the reason for her sadness.

The spring accents of the morning were sharp in his nostrils as he walked along the shaded lane. The acacia was in blossom, white and sweet. Here and there bobbed roses, all small; he could identify none of them. Varieties, he thought, so long out of favor in the cultivated world as to be virtually extinct. As, for that matter, was so much else from the lovely past.

And Ellery pondered painfully, as he walked, on the

Teacher's odd behavior. Surely a man with something to conceal would not have gone openly to the Potter for a replacement prayer jar so soon after the shattering of the old one? Or to the Weaver to have a new button sewn on his tunic?

And there was the question of time. While the Quenanites were not time-bound or time-harried, the Teacher could no more step out of the universal continuum than a man in Los Angeles or New York. Where had the old man been—what had he done—between 4:30, when he visited the Potter's workshop, and 4:55, when Ellery had found him in the meeting room over the body of the Storesman, while the people stood transfixed outside?

At 4:30 he had stepped into the Potter's shop for a new prayer jar, and obviously he had taken it at once to the sanquetum to place on the base where the broken jar had stood. This whole procedure could hardly have consumed more than five minutes. At 4:45 he had stepped into the Weaver's shop to have a new button sewn on; could this have taken more than five minutes also?

Ten minutes accounted for between 4:30 and 4:55 —ten out of twenty-five.

Leaving fifteen minutes not accounted for.

What had the old man done with them?

Still musing, Ellery came to the cottage of the Elders —the husband and wife who represented the old people of Quenan on the Crownsil. How old they were he could not imagine; he could only think of them as Adam and Eve, and he was sure that if he were able to examine them he would find them lacking navels.

Smiling toothlessly, they welcomed him; and the old woman patted the space beside her on the fleece-padded bench on which they sat soaking up the sun.

Them, at least, the tragedy seemed to have passed by. Perhaps they did not understand it, or had already forgotten it. He felt uncertain how to begin.

"You are here to help us," Adam broke the silence at last. "And we are thankful to you. Blessed be the Wor'd."

And Eve said, "Willy told us."

Ellery blinked. "Willy?"

"The Teacher. His name in the world was Willy." And the ancient lady nodded and smiled. A small thing, but astounding. The Teacher, that venerable, majestic figure out of the Old Testament, had once been a boy named Willy, wearing a lace collar and trundling a hoop with a stick along a wooden sidewalk!

"We have known him all our lives," said Adam.

"Then let me ask you," said Ellery. "Have you ever known him to lie?"

Neither replied. Perhaps they had gone back, in the manner of the very old, to some far-distant memory of flaring gas lamps and a harbor quilled with sharp white sails.

Then the old woman's withered lips trembled, and Ellery saw that the pair had simply been struck dumb by his question. "Lie?" she repeated. "The *Teacher?*"

And her husband rocked as if in pain. "Oh! Oh!"

And both began at once, in their unsteady voices, to impress on him the monstrousness of his question. The Teacher would never lie. He could not lie. Even about the most trifling matter.

"Not to save his life, Guest!" Adam exclaimed.

"Not to save his life!" Eve echoed.

Lines from some old book appeared magically in Ellery's head: Our master talks with the angels. "How do you know?" *He told us so.* "But perhaps he lies." *Fool! As though the angels would talk to a liar!*

But for some reason he could not pass their ancient testimony off with the usual smile as the product of senile delusion or narrow sectarian ignorance. All he knew —and the knowledge was a terror as well as a relief— was that he believed them without reservation or doubt.

The Teacher would not lie about even the most trifling matter.

The Teacher would not lie to save his life.

For the rest of the morning and afternoon, until the sun was well down in the western sky, Ellery pursued his investigations. The mill rasped, the waters rushed through their channels, the cattle lowed, and an old man testified in feeble, halting words. It was late in the afternoon when he returned to his room. The Superintendent was waiting for him.

"Guest," the Superintendent said, "the Teacher has instructed me, saying: 'Do you call upon the Guest and ask if he has any instructions. Do you then receive them and carry them out as if they came from me.'" He might have been reciting an inventory. "Accordingly," the Superintendent went on, "I have called upon you, Guest, and I ask if you have any instructions. I shall receive them and carry them out as if they came from the Teacher."

Ellery wanted to say nothing so much as, Yes, for God's sake get out of here and let me sleep a week, a month, a year.

What he actually said was: "Yes, Superintendent. Summon the Crownsil, the Teacher, the Successor, and yourself to the meeting hall in the Holy Congregation House for after the evening meal."

"I shall do so," said the Superintendent, and turned to go.

"Wait," said Ellery, and wondered why. "Aren't you the least curious, Superintendent, about my reasons for this summons?"

"I was not to ask for reasons, Guest, only for instructions."

"Ah, they could use you in Washington," sighed Ellery. "My reason is this, and you may tell them so: According to the laws and customs of Quenan, tonight they are to sit in trial."

It was quite dark in the long room. Candles had been lit by the Successor to reinforce the single lamp, but they seemed to Ellery to produce more shadows than light; they leaped and they danced and grew large and shrank away with every breath of wind let in by the opening door as the members of the Crownsil assembled. The darkness was palpable, he thought; it could be felt, a thing of shifting solids that the light of all the sun could not have melted.

While he waited for the people of the Crownsil to seat themselves about the long table, Ellery thought over the role he saw about to play. His to present, his to accuse, his to prosecute. Elroï the Procurator. The Devil's Advocate. (For that matter, was not Satan himself a prosecutor, accusing Job?) There had been murder most foul in Eden, and the task of arraignment, indictment, and pressure for judgment was now his—assigned him by the leader of the community, his authority to exercise it accepted by the council of the community.

What choice had they? There was no one else, no one at all, in Quenan with his knowledge of such things.

Again the guilty thought surfaced that he should be reporting the crime to the authorities of jurisdiction. But, really, who were they? In every respect but geography, Quenan lay outside the borders of the United States of America.

"The king's writ runs not in Connaught," said an old Irish proverb. Neither state nor federal power had ever "run" in the Valley of Quenan. And where no other governance obtained, it was the right of the people of any place—by the law of nations—to set up provisional powers . . . not merely their right, but their duty. And such powers, established here for so many decades, and exercised without question or molestation, could not even be deemed provisional any longer. (That this was all rationalization Ellery knew very well, in the part of him that remained Ellery; but in the part of him that had become Elroï, hazy with fatigue, misted over with sorrow, he paid no attention to it.)

Of one thing he—Ellery or Elroï—was sure: this was no kangaroo court, no rumor-ridden Star Chamber, no lynch mob. It was a high court of justice; and its bailiff was about to speak.

For the Superintendent had risen. "We are assembled," his flat, dry, uninflected voice intoned, "to sit in trial according to the laws and customs of Quenan." And he sat down; that was all.

To silence.

And the silence grew.

Ellery had expected questions, objections—something on which he could base his opening remarks. Were they trying to obstruct, to defeat him in the task they had in effect assigned to him, by the dead weight of their silence? Passive resistance? Dream-tired though he was, he felt annoyance. Why the delay? Reluctance to face facts, however prolonged, could not alter them.

But as the silence deepened he began to sense an identity between what he was now witnessing and the stillness of a Quaker meeting, or an Orthodox synagogue during silent prayer, or a mosque during that first moment while the faithful await the imam's invocation. And then it became a silence exceeding any of these, a silence so intense that he could not detect the slightest flutter of an eyelid or a nostril. It was as if they had all yielded to a yoga-like trance from which nothing but the last trumpet call would ever rouse them.

For a moment Ellery felt like those Gauls who, walking gingerly through the Rome they had just broken into, observed with an awe not so far from terror the white-bearded senators sitting so severely calm, so without movement, that the barbarians could only believe them to be demigods or statues . . .

He came to himself, the truth revealed. For slowly, gradually, as he stood there in that frozen room, with its utterly still company, the annoyance and restlessness and doubt seeped out of him, and the cloudy murk seemed to thin and lighten. And so Ellery came to understand the purpose of this time of concentrated quiet. It brought calm and peace into the room, and into the minds and hearts of all seated here.

Whereupon, once more, the Superintendent rose; but the Teacher, whose strange eyes were fixed on Ellery's face, did not look the Superintendent's way.

"Guest," the official said in a very different voice, the voice of man, not rote, "do you now tell us of the things you have learned and of the things you would have us do. And we shall listen, and we shall reflect, and we shall judge."

And he took his seat once more.

Ellery faced the robed figures around the long table with a great composure and tranquillity. (Not until later did he realize that this overriding feeling had been self-induced by something very like autohypnosis, serving not to dispel but to mask his extreme fatigue. He was feeling the illusive warmth of a man blissfully freezing to death.)

"Murder," he began, and immediately paused. Had a shudder run through them at the word—never before uttered in this room, the forecourt to a shrine dedicated to peace and love? Or had it been his imagination?

"Let me first tell you what murder is," Ellery said. "The life of a man was recently taken in this room" (and was there the slightest shift of every eye to the place on the floor where a new grass mat concealed the spilled blood, or had he—again—imagined it?) "and this man whose life was taken had not been charged with any crime, he had not been tried and convicted and sentenced to his death in the manner prescribed by law. The taking of human life without sanction or due process—that is murder. Storicai the Storesman was murdered."

They were grimly, violently still.

"Now before the facts of a murder can be ascribed to any person, there are three things which must be demonstrated to link the person accused or suspected with the crime.

"These three things are called opportunity, and means, and motive."

They did not yet understand, but they would. Ellery went on deliberately.

"Opportunity," he said, holding up a finger. "This is to say, when death results from a physical attack on the person of the victim—such as the slaying of the Storesman with a hammer—there must be evidence that the person accused or suspected was in fact present on the scene of the murder at or about the time it occurred, or that he *could* have been present.

"Means." Ellery held up a second finger. "This is to say, there must be evidence that the person accused or suspected had possession of, or had access to, the weapon with which the murder was committed.

"Motive." He held up a third finger. "This is to say, that it can be shown that the person accused or suspected had a reason for wishing to take the life of the victim."

He paused. Their faces were impassive but intent; whether they yet understood him it was too soon to judge.

"I shall try to prove opportunity first," Ellery said. "Will the Miller come forward and sit in this place?" He indicated a stool he had asked the Successor to put near the head of the table.

The Miller rose from the long bench and came forward. He was an oak of a man, gnarly, with a vast spread of shoulder. Flour dusted his reddish beard and rusty eyebrows. He breathed heavily as he sat down on the stool.

"What happened yesterday, Miller, when you had finished grinding?" Ellery asked him gently.

The man raised huge hands and rubbed them into his temples, as if they were millstones with which he would grind out the answers. In the loud voice of one accustomed to making himself heard above the splash of the millrace, the rasp of the stones, and the clatter of the sails, he said, "The first of the new flour," and stopped.

"What about the first of the new flour?"

The man looked surprised. "It was ready," he explained, as to a child. "I had sacked the first of the new flour. In a white sack, according to the way. Being the first of the new flour, it must be blessed. So I heaved it up on my shoulder"—he demonstrated awkwardly—"and I carried it here to the holy house for the Teacher to bless it."

"What time was that?"

Time? Just before 4:15. How did he know? He had observed the water clock as he left his mill.

"Very well. Now what did you do, Miller, when you carried the first sack of the new flour to the Holy Congregation House?"

The Miller started at him. "Why, I rang the bell, what else? But there was no answer, so of course I couldn't go in. With the Teacher not here—or surely he would have come to the door?—I had no reason to stay. I started to walk back to the mill."

"Started to?"

The Miller explained that he had walked only a short distance and had just turned into the trees when he heard footsteps and looked around. It was Storicai the Storesman, hurrying toward the holy house. "I was going to call out to him not to bother, that the Teacher was not there to answer the bell, bu before I could speak Storicai was at the door, looking all round like—like—"

"As if he did not wish to be seen?"

The Miller, who was not perspiring, nodded his gratitude. "That is so, Guest."

"Did Storicai see you?"

"I don't think so. I was in the shadows of the trees."

The shadows. The flaxen wicks smoldered. Wax ran down the candles and formed huge weepers. The shadows writhed.

"And what did Storicai do then, Miller?"

The man looked from face to face. His voice became hoarse, trembling on the brink of a shout. The Storesman had committed a *sin*. He had pulled open the door of the holy house without ringing the bell and he had entered without waiting to be admitted—in fact, when the Teacher had not been there to admit him.

"He committed a *sin*," the Miller repeated, knuckling his head.

"Thank you," said Ellery, and the big man went heavily back to his place. "Waterman?"

The Waterman rose and came forward. He was tall and young and sleek and graceful, walking with a glide; but his chief feature was wetness. His clothing showed more damp than dry, and his darkly bearded face and quick brown hands shone with moisture in the candle-light. He made Ellery think of a salamander.

"Yesterday afternoon," the Waterman answered Ellery's question, "I set out to clean the well across from the holy house. While I was in the well I heard the bell outside the holy house ring, and I started to climb up to ask whoever it was to lend me a hand in hauling up the bucket. But I slipped, and this made me slow. I heard the bellringer—I suppose now it must have been the Miller—I heard him go away. Then I heard someone else coming. I lifted my head above the housing of the well, and I saw . . ." He stopped to wipe his slick forehead with his slick hand.

"And you saw what, Waterman?" Ellery asked.

"It is as the Miller said. I saw Storicai go into the holy house. He did not ring the bell. He was not admitted by the Teacher."

Ellery glanced at the patriarch. The old man might have been alone in the long room, wrapped in an impenetrable silence. A great calm covered his face; his eyes, burning in the reflected light of the many candles, seemed fixed on something far away, a vision to which the stone walls of the holy house were no impediment.

Ellery felt the stirring of wonder. It was as if the Teacher did not care. Could he actually be indifferent to the purpose of this unprecedented proceeding? Or was it resignation?

"Waterman, what was the time when you observed Storicai enter the Holy Congregation House unlawfully?"

"It was about a quarter past the hour of four, Guest."

"Do you say this because that was the time fixed by the Miller, or because you knew of your own knowledge?"

"I knew of my own knowledge," the Waterman said quietly, "from the slant of the shadow made by the sun in the well."

"You may return to your place, Waterman." Ellery waited until the tall salamander had glided back to his seat on the bench. Then he addressed the motionless figures around the table. "It will be seen, then, that the Storesman is placed at the scene of his killing, by the testimony of the Miller and the Waterman, at a quarter past the hour of four. How long after he entered the holy house was he killed? Five minutes. This I know because the Storesman was wearing on his wrist a timepiece belonging to me, which I had lent him for the duration of my visit to Quenan. This timepiece, called a wrist watch, was broken by a blow of the hammer during the killing as Storicai flung up his hand to protect himself."

He took the wrist watch out of his pocket and held it up. "As you see, the hands stopped at twenty minutes past the hour of four—as I said, five minutes after the Storesman entered the holy house."

When he was satisfied that all had seen the position of the hands, he pocketed the watch and said, "I summon the Growther."

The Growther, or Grower, was middle-age. He was long in the body, like a cornstalk; and the skin under his fingernails was black from lifelong rooting in the earth. He spoke haltingly, in an eerie voice, as a plant might speak if it could be taught words.

Yesterday afternoon, the Growther said, he had visited the sick Slave. He had been with the Slave a quarter of an hour, praying with him and telling him of the crops. He had left the Slave's house when the Teacher arrived. He knew that the time he had come was three o'clock and the time he had left was a quarter past three because of the clock in the Slave's house.

And the Growther said, "Did you know, Guest, that inside the Slave's clock lives a little bird? At one time the bird would come out and call the hours. But it has not called the hours for a very long time."

"I did not know that, Growther," said Ellery gravely. "Thank you. And now, will the Herder come forward?"

The Herder was a knotty oldster with a great spreading beard. He squinted from under his bird's-nest brows as if into the sun; his skin was like the skin of a long-dried apricot. Try as Ellery would, he got nothing out of the whiskered mouth but bleats and grunts.

"What did you do yesterday afternoon, Herder?"

Bleat.

"Did you not visit the Slave's house?"

Grunt, accompanied by a nod.

"When did you step into the Slave's house?"

Grunt.

"Did you get there at four o'clock, or later?"

Bleat, untranslatable.

"Oh, all right," said Ellery. "Yesterday I understood you to say that you got there a bit before a quarter past four. Is that so?"

Nod.

"You found the Teacher there when you arrived?"

Nod.

"And the Teacher left the Slave's house at your coming?"

Nod.

"Immediately at your coming?"

Grunt, bleat, nod-nod.

"Thank you, that will be all." Ellery turned to the Teacher. "Can the Slave be brought here now?"

He saw now that, for all his distant look, the patriarch was attending the proceedings. For he nodded at once to the Successor, who hurried from the holy house. They must have had the Slave all ready to be brought in, because the door opened again a bare two minutes later to reveal the young Successor, sweating. He said something, and the Miller and the Waterman rose at once and stepped outside. They returned immediately carrying the Slave. Someone—perhaps the Carpentersmith —had rigged up a sort of reclining chair to which had been fixed two poles, making a crude palanquin; and in it half lay the ailing man.

The Successor swiftly indicated the spot near the foot of the table where the litter should be set down; the Miller and the Waterman set it down precisely there; then all three returned to their places.

The Slave looked as old as the Teacher was but did

not look. He looked like the southwestern hills—black-brown-red of skin with dry gullies for wrinkles over a skeleton of calcified bones, moribund as the desert itself. Only the Slave's eyes were alive—shining-black as a bird's eyes, and as unwinking. And this Slave, who was no longer slave, had the massive dignity of his blood; yes, and curiosity, too. The bird's eyes took in everything before they settled on Ellery's face.

"I thank you," said his echo of a voice; and Ellery knew that the whispering tones were giving him thanks for having him brought to the Holy Congregation House for his last Crownsil meeting. "And now I am ready."

"I will not tire you"—he had started to say "Slave," but the word had stuck in his throat—"for my questions are few," and Ellery quickly drew from the ancient man the story of his visitors of the day before, and confirmation of the times they had arrived at and departed from his house—the Growther, the Teacher, the Herder.

"Only one thing more," Ellery said gently. "You are ill, and you have had to lie in your bed. How can you have noted and remembered the times so exactly?"

It seemed to him that the smallest smile curved the withered lips. "There is so little time left to me," said the old Slave, "that I observe time as a young man observes his enemy."

"I need question you no further. And now if you wish to be taken back to your house—"

The ancient whispered, "I should like to remain," and glanced at the Teacher; and a look passed between them so intimate, so full of anguish and compassion that Ellery had to turn away.

And to the Crownsil he said, "And so we come to the Teacher's alibi."

"Al-i-bi?" repeated someone; and Ellery saw that it was the Superintendent. "This is not a word we have ever heard, Guest." And Ellery saw, from their faces, that it was so.

He explained it in the simplest terms he could evoke; and when he knew that they understood, he went on.

"We must therefore hold," Ellery said, "that the

Teacher's alibi ended when he stepped out of the—of the Slave's house, which was at fifteen minutes past four o'clock. It is only a few steps from the Slave's house to the Holy Congregation House; had the Teacher returned here from the Slave's house at once, he would have had to arrive just before twenty minutes past four, the time that the Storesman was struck down to his death. I have questioned everyone. No one remembers having seen the Teacher in the five minutes between fifteen and twenty minutes past four."

He did not look at the Teacher now.

"If anyone in this company now remembers having seen the Teacher, or has heard of another's having seen the Teacher, he must say so now."

And stopped. And waited. In the long room, no sound. Outside, no sound. In himself, no sound except the terrible beating of his heart.

He felt a tickle on his nose, descending; and he took out his handkerchief and wiped his streaming forehead. "It is thus established," Ellery said, "that the Teacher could have been here—in this room—on the scene of the slaying—at twenty minutes past four, the very moment that Storicai the Storesman was dealt the mortal blow."

No one coughed, shifted, snuffled, slewed about. They were turned to stone. What are you saying? their stone faces seemed to ask. What is your meaning? Because meaning your words must have, though to us they mean nothing.

It was as if the entire weight of the matter had been shifted to Ellery's shoulders. No one of them would help to move it from there one inch to the right or to the left, except as he might wrench their testimony from them.

So there was nothing to do but turn to the source.

To the Teacher, Ellery said painfully, "Teacher, did you go directly from the Slave's house to this holy house yesterday?"

And the old man's eyes came back from the far place and looked at him; and he said calmly, "It is so, Quenan."

Now was there something heard in that room, a many-lunged sigh, of which one part was his own. Ellery said, "And were you then already in the holy house *before* Storicai was slain with the hammer?"

"It is so, Quenan."

And again the assembled sigh.

Ellery knew light-headedness. He pressed his palms on the long table, leaning. How theatrical this all was, how pompously unnecessary. Why had he called upon the trappings of interrogation, Crownsil, witnesses, the whole dismal reconstruction of the timetable of the Teacher's movements? When all he had had to do was ask the patriarch the simple question, *Did you kill Storicai, Teacher?* to get the truthful answer. The Teacher did not lie. The Teacher would not lie.

Ellery actually turned to the old man and opened his mouth before reason took control again. Whatever the cause—the other-worldliness of the place, the strangeness of the people, his own enervation, the headiness of the encroaching desert—he had hardly been the same man since setting foot here. A case that rested solely on an accused's bearing witness against himself was not a civilized proceeding; it was an inquisition. This was not a matter between Teacher and Guest, a duel of antagonists. This was a searching after truth. For what is truth? *If you will be persuaded by me, pay little attention to Socrates, but much more to the truth, and if I appear to you to say anything true, assent to it, but if not, oppose me with all your might, taking good care that in my zeal I do not deceive both myself and you, and like a bee depart, leaving my sting behind.* And then there were the Crownsil and the people to persuade. Truth might touch their hearts through faith; but in such a dreadful matter it must convince their minds as well, and that could only come through evidence.

Ellery looked away from the Teacher to the faces around the table.

"Storicai is established as having entered this holy house at fifteen minutes past four. He is established as having been struck down to his death at twenty minutes past four. And the Teacher is established as having been here between Storicai's entering and Storicai's dying. And these two things establish that the Teacher had the *opportunity* to commit the crime. But not these two things alone establish his opportunity. There is another thing to support them."

From his pocket he took the glassine envelope containing the metal button he had found in Storicai's hand. "This button I removed from the Storesman's dead hand," he said. "I shall pass it among you, so that you may look at it closely, and know it for what it is." And he handed it to the Superintendent, who took it and passed it to the Successor as if it burned; and Ellery watched the button go around the table, quickly, leaving pain behind it.

And when it had been returned to him, Ellery said, "The very presence of this metal button in the slain man's hand is witness to its meaning. The threads still clinging to it are witness that it was torn away by Storicai, from the garment to which it was sewn, during the struggle that cost the Storesman his life . . . torn away from the garment of the person with whom he was struggling—who else?"

And Ellery said, sickening himself as he said it, "And this places the owner of the button on the scene of the slaying at the very moment of its taking place. And who, alone in Quenan, wears metal buttons on his garments? And who, in fact, had a metal button replaced on his garment?"

Someone made a stifled sound.

"I call the Weaver to witness."

She came slowly, chin on her bosom; nor would she sit, but remained standing before the stool. Once more it was necessary for him to phrase the answer as well as the question: yes, she did sew a button, a new metal button with the sacred *N* upon it, on the Teacher's robe at fifteen minutes before five o'clock—only twenty-five minutes after the murder. Her "yes" was torn from her. And she returned, with the step of an old woman, to her place.

Ellery felt his own legs trembling. He had to steel himself in order to turn to the Teacher.

"Do you then admit, Teacher, that this button found in Storicai's dead hand came from your garment?"

And calmly the Teacher answered, "It is so."

Ellery looked about, and he saw that he had company indeed in his distress. The stone had crumbled from their faces; each sat exposed in his knowledge and his grief.

And on those naked faces sat not knowledge and grief alone. For there was fear as well. Fear for themselves? No . . . no. It was for the Teacher. They had grown greatly afraid for their Teacher.

And Ellery forced his glance again at that old man, and what he saw shook him more than had he seen its opposite. For on that etching face, the face of the all-but-accused, sat a serenity that could only have come from purest peace within.

And, hating himself, Ellery looked away.

"We now," he said, and paused to still his crawling flesh, "we now weigh the second of our three measures of guilt—Means."

To set the scales, he reconstructed the *res gestae* leading up to the crime—the thefts of the Teacher's key in the night, the evidence of an attempt to enter the sanquetum with a faulty duplicate key, and so on—and the clues incident to the murder itself. He described the wounds on the dead Storesman's head, both at the back and in the forehead. He told them of the specks of baked clay in the dead Storicai's hair; of the bloody hammer beside the body; of the duplicate key in Storicai's pocket; of the unlocked door to the sanquetum; of the prayer jar that did not quite fit its base; of the disturbed columns of coins in the arque, and of the purple shard he found under the arque, and of the bloodstain on a corner of the arque.

"Let me sum up for you what all this means," Ellery said. "The Storesman had secretly made a duplicate key to the sanquetum in order to enter the room forbidden to him, as to all others but the Teacher. He could have had only one purpose in doing this—to steal the treasure of Quenan. He came to the door of the holy house, he looked about, he did not see that the Miller and the Waterman were observing him, and he entered without announcement or permission. In the holy house, he hurried to the door of the forbidden room, and unlocked it with the duplicate key he had made, and went in, and began to take the silver coins from the arque.''

They were all leaning toward him now, eagerly, like plants toward the sun.

"At this moment a person—let me call him Witness —a Witness noticed the open sanquetum door and someone within, approached the room, saw the Storesman in the act of stealing the treasure, and in outraged anger plucked one of the scroll-filled prayer jars from its base and raised it high and brought it down on Storicai's head—the back of the head, since the Witness struck from behind. The jar shattered, shards of it falling all around, and one of the shards fell under the arque. Storicai collapsed under the blow, and in falling struck the back of his head on a corner of the arque."

Their sigh made a long, low hissing in the meeting room.

"Now this Witness," said Ellery, "must have then run from the sanquetum, perhaps to call for help. But almost at once the Storesman recovered from the blow by the prayer jar, leaped to his feet, and desperate to prevent the Witness's outcry against him, ran after the Witness, caught up with him here—near this table—grappled with him and, I have no doubt, in his frenzy of fear at being discovered in the act of sacrilege, tried to kill the Witness. And so they struggled in a terrible silence, and during the struggle the Witness managed to snatch the hammer which the Teacher had left for the Successor on this table, and in defense of his life swung it as Storicai. Storicai flung up his arm, and the first blow smashed my wrist watch on his arm, stopping it at twenty minutes past four. The second blow struck Storicai on the forehead. There was no need for a third."

A bit of burning wick detached itself and floated down to the pool of liquefied wax from which the flame rose. Here it continued to burn, separately, as if it had separate life.

"This, then, is a picture of the crime," Ellery continued. "Now for what happened immediately thereafter. Let us proceed step by step. The first thing the Witness must have done after slaying the Storesman was to return to the sanquetum, in order to restore the room to its former undisturbed state. To do this he had to collect the pieces of the broken prayer jar and dispose of them —and in doing so, he overlooked one shard under the arque—and also to replace the broken jar with a whole one and refill it with the scattered scrolls.

"Now, who did this?

"I ask the Potter to come forward."

The Potter came forward, no longer the Shavian figure he had first appeared. His feet dragged as if they bore a crushing weight. He lowered himself to the stool painfully.

"Someone came to you yesterday for a prayer jar to replace one which had been broken. Who, Potter?"

The Potter's slip-specked beard trembled, and he opened his mouth. But nothing came out.

"Who, Potter?" Tension made Ellery's own voice sound brutal.

This time a strangled noise emerged. But it was a noise without meaning.

"Who, Potter?" shouted Ellery.

And so at last the anguished words were torn from the Potter's throat: "The Teacher! The Teacher . . . !"

And now a soft keening rose, like a mournful wind, and Ellery, who could have keened with them, waited until it died away. And no eye turned to the Teacher, not even Ellery's.

"And what was the time when the Teacher came to your shed and asked for a new prayer jar for the sanquetum, Potter?"

"At half past the hour of four."

"Ten minutes after Storicai was struck dead," Ellery said, and slowly waved, and the Potter stumbled back to his place.

"Thus we have connected the Teacher," Ellery resumed after a moment, "with the first weapon used, the weapon that merely stunned—the sanquetum jar. Now let us consider the second weapon used, the weapon that took Storicai's life—the hammer." And he reached down and took from the floor, where he had laid it, the wrapped hammer; and he began to unwrap it, and the cloth stuck in the now dry blood, and he had to tear it away as they shuddered. And the bloodstains on the hammer's head were still to be seen.

"Listen to me," Ellery said. "Yesterday in this room I took the imprint of the fingertips of all present—the dead Storesman, the Teacher, the Successor, the Superintendent, and the eleven members of the Crownsil of Twelve still living. Do you remember?"

Oh, yes, they remembered; they could not forget *that* mystery within a mystery; so much was clear. But did they have any idea of the significance of fingerprints?

"Do you know why I made each of you press your fingertips on the ink pad and then on the white paper?"

They were blanks.

"Then I will tell you," Ellery said. "Each man here, and each of the women, too, lift up your hands and look at the tips of your fingers." The time they glanced at one another doubtfully; but the Chronicler raised his hands and looked at them, and one by one the others did likewise. "Look closely. Do you see the little lines and loops and whorls in your skin, making up a certain pattern?" There was a concert of nods. "This pattern can be transferred from your fingertips to another surface, especially a smooth dry one. Surely you have all seen the imprint of your fingers, or of the children's, on a wall or a window?"

"This we know, Elroï," the Chronicler spoke up suddenly. "But what is the meaning of it?"

"The meaning of it, Chronicler, is that the fingertips of no two people in the world leave the same picture—

no, not even those of twins born of the same egg. In the outside world the fingerprints of millions and millions of people of all nations and races and colors have been collected, and not once have those of one person been found to match exactly those of another. Thus it may be said that each human being carries about with him—from his birth to his death and beyond, until the body all but crumbles into dust—a set of marks or signs on his fingers by which he, and he alone, can be told from all others in the world. Now do you grasp my meaning?"

It seemed that they did not; at least, on no face turned up to his did he see anything but a brow-knotted struggle to understand. Or was it a struggle to believe? For this might well come down to a matter, not of comprehension, but of faith.

"You must believe me when I say that it is true," said Ellery. "I, Elroï Quenan, whose coming in a time of great trouble was foretold." And may God forgive me, he thought, for *that*. "So now we come to the weighing of the Means, and to weigh that we must first throw into the balance the fingerprints."

He held up the bloodied hammer, grasping it by the edges of the head and the bottom of the grip.

"You will see that I have dusted the gripping surface of the hammer with a white powder; and that this white powder, when blown gently away, has left a residue on the fingerprints made by the hand that grasped it in slaying the Storesman, thus revealing a picture of them."

He laid the hammer carefully down on the table and reached for his fingerprinting kit. The prints on the hammer showing white against the darkened wood of the grip, he took out a piece of black paper. "Teacher, will you allow me to take the fingerprints of your right hand?"

And now the silence could be scratched, it was so hard. But the Teacher wore the same expression of serenity.

"It shall be as you say, Elroï," he said.

Ellery took the old hand; it was warm and quiet in his. *If I forget thee, O Jerusalem . . .* He rolled the patriarch's fingers, then brought out the prints with white powder. He laid the black paper beside the hammer, and produced his pocket lens.

"I wish you all to rise and, one at a time, to look through the glass at the fingerprints of the Teacher you have just seen me take, and then at the fingerprints of the slayer on the hammer. And you will see that the fingerprints on the one are identical with the fingerprints on the other."

But—would they? Primitive people who had never laid eyes on a photograph were often unable to recognize the most familiar people or objects snapped by a camera. There might be a similar blindness here. And indeed, while the Crownsil and the others filed by and examined the two exhibits in turn through the lens, while a few nodded, most shook their heads. Nevertheless, he waited until they were all seated again, and said, "Thus, from the prints of the Teacher's fingertips on the hammer, we know that the Teacher, and only the Teacher, could have used the hammer to slay the Storesman. It is proved."

But was it? To them?

The whole suffocating mantle of fatigue dropped over him again, so that he had to fight his way free of it. And Ellery turned to the serene old man, to prove his guilt by evidence they would have no choice but to accept.

"Teacher," he said abruptly, "was it you who gathered together the pieces of the broken prayer jar, you who went directly from this holy house after the slaying to the Potter's for a new jar?"

And the old man answered, "It is so, Elroï."

"And was it your right hand that held this hammer?"

This time there was the least pause before the Teacher, still serenely, answered, "It is so, Elroï."

A gush of brash leaped into Ellery's mouth, and he had to swallow the burning stuff before he could say: "So we have established that the Teacher had opportunity to kill the Storesman—that is, that he was here; and that he had the means—that is, that his hand grasped the hammer.

"Now we must weigh the third and last measure of guilt—Motive."

And Ellery said:

"In stealing the Teacher's key to the sanquetum door and from it making a duplicate key, Storicai sinned in intent. But, having made the key, he proceeded to sin in fact. He committed three acts of offense against Quenan and the Teacher who had taught him.

"Storicai entered the holy house without ringing the bell and without being admitted by the Teacher—this was the first offense. He entered the forbidden room, which the Teacher alone among you has the right to enter—this was the second offense. And he laid greedy hands on the treasure—and this was his third offense.

"So, in the space of five shameful minutes, Storicai the Storesman offended against you, his brothers in Quenan, in general, and against his and your Teacher, in particular. Surely you can understand that the Teacher, venerable and wise and revered though he is, is still a man of flesh and blood, subject to the same weaknesses that beset us all? That, catching Storicai in the act of committing three sins against the laws and customs of Quenan, your Teacher was seized with a great wrath and rose up against the transgressor with whatever instrument lay at hand—a prayer jar, a hammer—and struck down him who had wrought blasphemy upon the Wor'd?"

He looked up and down the two lines of faces, sure that now, at last, he would see agreement written there, even relief. But he saw only the same confused and fearful people.

What was the matter?

Ellery said in muttered, cracking tones, "And now I really cannot hold off any longer asking the question— the question of questions."

And the Teacher said, "Seek the truth and we shall be—"

There was a word after "be," but Ellery was not sure

he had heard it correctly. Had the old man said "safe"? Or was it "saved"?

Well. No matter. Now for it. Ellery braced himself. "Teacher. Did you slay Storicai the Storesman?"

The patriarch replied instantly, and his reply staggered Ellery . . . made him reach for the table, and support himself.

The rich voice of the Teacher said, "It is you who say it."

They had been gathered at the foot of the long table in a group, deliberating, praying, debating in low voices, for a long time. A final disagreement, apparently irreconcilable, sent the Chronicler as spokesmen to the Superintendent, to whisper in his ear.

That dry man immediately nodded and approached Ellery.

"I am asked to tell you, Elroï, that some of the Crownsil are confused by the pictures on the hammer, what you call the fingerprints. These persons say: Elroï says that the fingerprints on the hammer are the very same as the Teacher's fingerprints on the paper, but we could not be sure that all those little lines and loops are the same in both, so how can he? In a matter as grave as this, there must be no doubt. This is what they have asked the Chronicler to ask me to ask you, and this is what I ask you now."

Ellery turned wearily to the Successor, who had sat like a piece of petrified wood throughout most of the proceedings.

"Will you please bring me some paper?" He had to repeat his question, for the Successor seemed as deaf as stone, too; but then the young man roused with a start, blushed deeply, and scuttled to the scriptorium to return in a moment with the paper.

Ellery distributed the paper, one sheet to each member of the Crownsil. They were only ten now, for the Slave had been returned to his house, too ill to remain longer in the meeting hall.

After going around the table from member to member, taking the prints of each, Ellery said, "Each person at the table now has before him a sheet of paper on which are impressed the prints of his own fingers. I ask you to do the following: Each of you is to write on his paper, beneath his fingerprints, a secret mark. It may be anything you choose—a circle, a little tree, a cross-mark, anything you wish. Do not tell me or show me which mark you are making." He dipped into his kit and tossed a few pencils on the table. "You may pass the pencils among you. Now I shall turn my back, so that I cannot see what you are doing." He turned his back. "Now do you all make your secret marks on your papers, and be sure you remember which mark you have made."

He stood there patiently, in a sort of exhausted wonder at the extraordinary situation in which he found himself. Behind him arose a sound made of shuffling feet, heavy breathing, and the rustling of clothes.

"Is it done?"

There was a little added confusion. Then the voice of the Superintendent said, "It is done."

Ellery did not turn around. "Now, Superintendent, do you collect the papers."

After a moment the superintendent said, 'It is done. I have collected the papers."

"You will now shuffle them, Superintendent, placing them in random order, so that I cannot possibly guess from their order which paper belongs to whom."

After a few moments the Superintendent said, "And that is done, Elroï."

Ellery turned around; the ten sheets lay in a neat pile at the head of the table. Under their puzzled eyes he pulled the stool over, sat down, and took from his pocket the fifteen sets of fingerprints he had recorded the day before, each labeled with the title of the official whose prints it bore. He picked up the top sheet of the unidentified set he had just taken, and compared it with the top sheet of the identified set. They did not match, and he went on to the second sheet of the identified set. Then to the third. The fourth sheet of the old set was the one he was looking for.

He held up the sheet of unidentified prints with the secret mark. For effect, he did not speak at once. They were all watching his lips breathlessly.

"I have here a paper bearing fingerprints and a secret mark. The secret mark is an arrangement of eight lines, forming a square within a square. I say to you, without any doubt, that the fingerprints on this paper were made by"—and he turned suddenly to a pair of startled female eyes—"you, Weaver! Is it so? Tell it aloud, Weaver —are these your prints?"

"Yes," the woman breathed, "for the square within a square is the secret mark I made."

A murmur of amazement arose from the long table. Ellery stilled it with a gesture.

"I have only begun," he said; and he began comparing the second sheet from the secret-mark pile with his master set. Again the holding of breaths. Again his deliberate prolongation of the suspense. And then Ellery said, holding up the sheet, "The prints on this paper are marked with a wavy line such as children draw when they wish to represent water. The maker of this water sign is trying to mislead me, I fear. For one would expect the secret mark of water to be made by the Waterman. But it was not. *It was made by you, Chronicler.* Tell it! These are your fingerprints, I say."

And the Chronicler, scratching his beard as if caught in a sly joke, nodded. "They are mine, Elroï, even as you say."

After that, there was nothing to it. The Waterman had drawn a little house; the Growther had put down two interlocking circles; the Potter had made three Xs; the Miller had scratched the outline of an animal Ellery guessed was intended as a cow only because of its enormous udders; and so on.

"So you may see," he said, when he had finished, "that there can be no mistake when the fingerprints are compared by the eye of one who knows how to read them. The fingerprints on the hammer came from the hand of the Teacher."

They were convinced. He did not look at the patriarch, who had sat in total silence throughout the demonstration.

Once again they withdrew to their deliberations, closing in together at the other end of the table. Once again Ellery looked at them through clouded eyes, his face supported by trembling hands. Presently the Weaver began to cry. And then the Chronicler rose and with a reluctant gesture beckoned the Superintendent. He spoke in so low a voice that the man had to stoop to hear.

The Superintendent slowly, very slowly, returned to Ellery, and as the pale man stood before him Ellery forced himself to speak.

"What is their verdict?" he asked. "If they have reached one." For in that moment it seemed to him the ultimate folly to imagine that they would find against their leader. It had all been a futile farce.

"They have reached a verdict," said the Superintendent hoarsely. His eyes were starting from his head. "It is the verdict of all, with no nay-sayers. The Teacher is guilty of the death of Storicai the Storesman."

His self-control wilted suddenly. And he crouched and slapped his hands over his face, rocking and crying.

Like a signal, it touched off a remarkable demonstration. The two women of the Crownsil, the Weaver and the ancient female of the pair of Elders, burst into wails, the old woman tearing at her hair and beating her breasts with her withered fists. Tears sprang from the eyes of the men and fell into their beards. Some laid their heads on the table, clawing at it with both hands while they wept.

But of the entire company it was the young Successor who sobbed most heartbrokenly. His sturdy body twitched and jumped as if nothing, nothing in this world or the next, could ever make him whole again.

And it was the Teacher who consoled him, who laid a gently urgent hand on the boy's racked shoulder, who then stroked his hair and murmured in his ear, making little soothing sounds as if to a terror-stricken child. And gradually the Successor's sobs lessened, and became a whimper, and the whimper died; and Ellery looked around to find that all had fallen silent.

And he turned again to the Superintendent. "And the sentence? The judgment?"

The man peered through red, swimming eyes. "Although the decision of the Crownsil, once made, may not be revoked, it can pass neither sentence nor judgment."

"Then who—?" Ellery began stupidly.

The Superintendent whispered, "Only the Teacher."

My God, he thought, my God. He had forgotten!

And the Teacher straightened and faced them; and the others rose as one; and the Teacher made a gesture of benediction, and they took their sets once more. And there was silence.

"Blessed is the Wor'd," began the old man, "over all the earth and unto all mankind that dwell hereon. Very many have been the blessings of the Wor'd unto me. My years have been long, my wives and children and children's children many. But even had I not enjoyed such riches, I would be rich still. For, blessed be the Wor'd, I have enjoyed other riches beyond number—the rain and the rainbow; the sun and the stars; the holy breath that is the wind. Blessed be the Wor'd for the sight and sound of birds; for the song in the voices of women; for the sweat on the bodies of men earned through toil; for the antelope in its flight and the smiling talk of friends; for the scent of grasses and the feel of watered earth; for the upturned faces of suckling lambs, and the peace that comes from prayers, and the grain that makes good bread; for the thousand perfumes of the flowers, and their thousand colors; for the shade of trees, and the happy agony of birth, and for children's voices.

"Blessed be the Wor'd," said the Teacher, and his voice rang through the meeting room, "for I say to you that no man can abide upon the earth so long as to grow weary of its riches. The moon must wane in its time, and vanish; but after the darkness comes the new moon, glorious."

And the old man paused. And then he said, in quite a different voice, "This is my judgment, this is my sentence that I pass upon myself:

"Tomorrow, at the sun's setting, I shall be caused to cease from among you"—did that quiet voice falter just a little?—"according to the manner decreed by the law."

For a second—one second of bottomless horror during which Ellery felt that he must surely burst, and everything whirled before his eyes in great and roaring circles—for one second no one made a sound.

But then the Successor cried out, "No!" in fearful disbelief, and again, *"No!"* And the womanly voice of the Weaver joined in anguished lamentation.

"Stop now, do you now stop at once, for you trouble not yourselves alone, but me." And the utterance, so firm and gently said, silenced them more quickly than a shout. "Do not grieve," the Teacher said, "for it must be. It is thus written, and only thus it is written, and as it is written so must it come to pass. Blessed is the Wor'd."

For weeks, months, Ellery had been starved for rest. But that night he could not sleep even for a moment. Something was *wrong*—every cell in his exhausted brain told him so. And yet he could not see what, he could not think where. Had the very simplicity of the case made him careless? Blindly unable to see the forest for the trees?

He tossed and shivered and perspired while the deep-seated pain settled deeper.

At the bottom it became a choice between the little bottle of red capsules and giving up. He gave up.

He crawled from the pallet, and switched on his flashlight, and then decided to save the battery; so he lit the candles in the earthenware candlesticks—salt-glazed, he noticed, grimacing at the detail.

Detail, detail—somewhere existed a detail he had overlooked. It gnawed away at him like the fox at the Spartan boy's belly. He had to organize, he had to organize his thoughts. Something about the trial, the end of the trial . . . no, not the end exactly, but toward the end . . . something there; that was what was bothering him. While he was talking about motive? Had his primer exposition of motivation been faulty? Had he left something out? Was that it?

As he continued to think about it, pulling on a jacket against the chilly desert night, tucking his feet back under the blanket, Ellery's heart sank even lower. For, granted that Storicai had been guilty of great sins against Quenan; granted that the Storesman had committed the community's first crime in almost two generations; granted also that religious belief sometimes assumed sudden spasmodic forms of fanaticism (a pilgrim to Mecca had only recently been torn to pieces by maddened worshipers for having, in a fit of sickness, vomited on the holy Kaaba): granted, granted, granted. Still . . . would the Teacher have so lost command of himself—that most patient and disciplined of men—as to yield to an impulse of violence? The Teacher guilty of violence?—that saintliest of the brothers?

As for the possibility that the old man had struck, not in a fit of rage, but with coldly predetermined intention, Ellery could not for a moment credit it.

But certainly he had here got to the root of his hag-mounted doubts: the motive, which had seemed so utterly convincing during the trial, was now not convincing at all. The Teacher was a man whose nature excluded a resort to violence; who would not, who *could* not, have struck Storicai with the prayer jar. The prayer jar! How could Ellery have believed for a moment that the holy man would desecrate a sacred vessel, even to smite a sinner?

And the hammer—would the Teacher have been capable of swinging it at even the meanest of his flock? Not once, but twice? A hammer, a skull-crushing *hammer?* Even in self-defense? Even to save the life that he himself had condemned to be taken tomorrow?

Unthinkable. It was unthinkable.

Think it through again, think it through . . .

And the questions came crowding, elbowing one another, in their release from the dark cell in which he had imprisoned them.

Why had the Teacher left such a plain trail to himself? For that was what he had done:

Ten minutes after Storicai's death the old man had shown up at the Potter's shed to ask for a new scroll jar.

Fifteen minutes later he had gone openly to the Weaver to have his "lost"—his unique, his identifiable —button replaced.

And how was it that, having meticulously swept up the fragments of the broken jar in the sanquetum, the Teacher had overlooked one shard? A shard that Ellery had seen almost at once . . .

And the manner of his responses to the direct questions. Asked if he had gone straight from the Slave's house to the Holy Congregation House, the old man had answered, *It is so.* Asked if he had been in the holy house just before Storicai was struck down, he had answered, *It is so.* Asked if the button found in the dead man's hand had come from his garment, he had answered, *It is so.* Asked if it was he who had gathered together the broken pieces of the prayer jar, if it was he who had gone from the holy house after the killing to the Potter's for a replacement jar, the old man had answered, *It is so.* Asked if it was his hand that had held the hammer, he had answered, *It is so.*

But asked if he had killed the Storesman, he had *not* answered, *It is so.* He had answered: *It is you who say it!*

It is you who say it was not at all the same as *It is so.* The Teacher did not lie—no, as the Elders had both cried out, not even to save his life. *It is you who say it* had been the equivocation of a man who could not lie, but who at the same time did not want to tell the truth, the whole truth.

Therefore . . . therefore (and Ellery shivered in the cold room, made colder by his thoughts) the whole truth has not yet been told. He would have to begin again.

The moment he re-examined the button, with its mystic *N* in the candlelight, Ellery saw what he had failed to see before, and cursed himself for his blindness.

The ends of the thread on the button were not raggedly torn, as they would have been had they been ripped away in a struggle. Instead, under the lens they showed up sharp and clean. They had been severed from the garment with a knife or scissors.

He turned the button over. The lens immediately showed him another proof of his carelessness—criminal carelessness, he told himself bitterly. There was a fresh-looking little gash where the oxidized surface of the soft metal had suffered a recent scratch, as if a sharp-edged instrument had slipped while cutting the thread.

My God, Ellery said to himself wildly, I investigate what I think is a primitive crime in a primitive setting of primitive people, and I find a sophisticated *frame-up!* The button was deliberately cut from the Teacher's robe! The button was deliberately planted in the dead man's hand!

But thank God it was not too late.

Ellery sprang from the pallet and began to dress. He must be thorough now, careful not to underestimate his adversary. The Teacher's life was at stake. The Teacher, who was prepared to sacrifice his life rather than expose the evil—the really evil—sinner in his flock.

By some magic Ellery's brain was now clear. His first morning in Quenan leaped from his memory to awareness: the Teacher in the storehouse, exchanging his broken pocketknife for a new one . . .

Ellery blew out the candles, and seizing the flashlight he made his way through the little settlement in the cold sweetness of the night. The wind was rushing through the trees. There was no light behind any window, but Ellery was certain that vigil, in the darkness, was being kept throughout the town.

At the Holy Congregation House he hesitated. He was excused from having to ring the bell and await admittance; why did he always hesitate? Perhaps because I am so fallible, he thought; and he went in.

He groped through the meeting hall to the Teacher's chamber. The light from the lamp over the sanquetum door, making the interior of the patriarch's room just visible, touched the old man's serene face, his open eyes. He was stretched out on his pallet in the middle of the room, hands behind his head, gazing up at the ceiling as through a window . . . as if he saw clearly the great stars wheeling and blazing in the black heavens.

He did not move or speak when Ellery came in. He knows I'm here, Ellery thought, and he's not surprised. Has he been expecting me?

There were pegs symmetrically spaced on either side of the door, and from one of them hung the Teacher's outer garment. Ignoring the old man on the bed, Ellery searched the robe for hidden pockets. He found the side slits, and in the depths of one of them he found what he was looking for.

It was the Teacher's knife, the new one he had procured in the storehouse under Ellery's eyes—in a wooden sheath, bone-handled, the sheath and knife held together by a leather thong. He switched on his flashlight and slipped the knife out of the sheath and examined the blade closely.

And there it was—a nick on the cutting edge, near the point. And caught in the nick was a tiny sliver of metal, the same soft metal of the button.

Not only had the button been deliberately severed from the Teacher's robe, it had been severed by the Teacher's knife!

And Ellery raised his eyes to that long quiet body, but there was no sign in it of perturbation, or even concern. The old man continued to stare through the ceiling, although he knew well enough what Ellery had done and seen.

Ellery softly left the Teacher's room and the holy house and made his way back through the wind and the *weedit, weedit* of the frogs to his quarters. And there he picked up the hammer and re-examined it. One item of planted evidence he had already exposed—the button.

Was it possible that the hammer, too, showed evidence of the frame-up of the Teacher?

In this shifted frame of reference, it seemed to him now that the hammer seemed too new-looking—rather, too unused-looking—to have justified the Teacher's reference to it, during Ellery's talk with him after the discovery of the Storesman's body, as "the hammer from my tool chest."

He dipped a corner of the toweling provided him into the ewer of water and carefully rubbed away the bloodstains on the striking surface of the hammer. He had been right. There were no abrasions or scratches on the metal of the head. This hammer had never been used for hammering nails or any other ordinary purpose. Was it possible that there had been an exchange of hammers? But if this was a new hammer it had most likely come from the storehouse. Then perhaps the Teacher's . . .

Once again Ellery made his way through the dark lanes of the hamlet, this time to the supply building. He needed no key; it was secured against marauding animals by an inside latch, and to release it he had merely to put his hand through a hole in the door made for the purpose.

It seemed to him that already the storehouse was filled with the effluvium of neglect. They had better elect another Storesman soon, he thought, or this place will begin to smell like a grave. He had to make an effort to pull his mind back to his mission.

Flashing his light among the bins and barrels and shelves, he finally located the compartment where the hammers were stored.

There were only three. Using a handkerchief, he examined them. Two were clearly new; one showed definite signs of use.

Is this used one the real murder weapon? Ellery asked himself. If so, someone had switched hammers after the crime—cleansed this one of Storicai's blood, placed it with the new ones in the storehouse, taken one of the new ones, dipped it in the still-wet blood of the victim, and then set it beside the body.

But why? How did the exchange of hammers compound the frame-up of the Teacher (who had certainly, at some point, become aware of the frame-up)? Why? Why?

And the question rang over and over in Ellery's head until he was sick with it . . .

He returned to his quarters carrying both hammers, thinking of samurai wearing two swords to signify their rank; of fighting priests in the Dark Ages, forbidden to use swords, going into battle against the heathen and laying about them with the *martels-de-fer*, the great fighting mallets; and of other strange and useless things.

Once more he opened his fingerprint kit and set to work. And tested the hammer he had taken from the storehouse, and found fingerprints. The fingerprints of two people, as he expected. And, in dread, he compared them with his master set of fifteen.

And when he saw whose prints they were, the disjointed pieces of the truth fell into place, and sickened him.

For the second time that night, Ellery entered the patriarch's room. Nothing had changed. The old man was still unmoving, still untroubled. Had he placed himself in a kind of mystical trance? But the first assertion Ellery made (with such difficulty!) the Teacher answered at once. And their interchange began to form a sort of litany, as if an act of worship were being performed in that bare dim chamber.

"It was you, Teacher, who cut the button off your robe with your knife and placed the button in the dead man's hand."

"Yea."

"It was you who took the killing hammer to the storehouse and cleansed it, and left it there, and brought back another hammer, and stained its head in the Storesman's blood, and placed it beside the body."

"Yea."

"You deliberately left a trail by way of the Potter and the Weaver which could lead only to yourself."

"Yea."

"You wished me to find evidence against you and against no other."

"Yea."

And Ellery, holding his voice down with all his strength, asked, "Why, Teacher, in heaven's name, *why?*"

"For thus it is written," said the Teacher.

" 'It is written, it is written!' Where are all these things written?"

It seemed to him the old man's beard lifted a little in a smile. "It is written in the book which was lost; or it is written in a book yet to be; or it may be written in the book which is Earth itself and all who dwell upon it, and in which all things were, and are, and will be written."

"Let us rather speak of what I can understand, Teacher," Ellery cried. "It is now clear to me that you *wished* to be accused of the Storesman's murder—that you *wished* to stand trial—that you *wished* to be declared guilty. Is that not so?"

And the old man calmly replied, "I am guilty."

"But not of striking the blow that slew the man!"

And the old man was silent. And then he sighed, and he said, "Nay, not of striking the blow."

"Then you are shielding him who actually struck it!"

And again the Teacher did not reply at once, and again he sighed, and again he finally said, "It is so, Elroï."

"So you know who slew Storicai?"

The majestic head nodded. "It is written that thus it would come to pass."

"I do not know about that, Teacher. I do know that on the true weapon, the hammer that actually crushed out Storicai's life, I found the fingerprints of the slayer. They are the fingerprints of—shall I say the name?"

"Said or unsaid, the Wor'd is sure."

"That does not say it. Therefore I must. Storicai was killed by the Successor."

Now for the first time the patriarch shifted his eyes to Ellery's face. "Elroï," he said, "before your coming

here I knew nothing of fingerprints. But this I knew—
that the Successor had handled the hammer. And I was
afraid that, in some mysterious way beyond my knowledge, it could be shown that it was he indeed who had
struck with the hammer, and that therefore it would be
safer for the boy if that hammer were not found by the
body. So I cleansed it and in its place set one which had
been in my hand but not in his. Alas. I should have
known that deceit is always undone."

Not always, old man, Ellery said; but not aloud.

Aloud he said: "Am I right, then, in what I have only
now come to believe, Teacher? You returned from the
Slave's house to this holy house just in time to see the
killing of Storicai at twenty minutes past four—in time to
see, but too late to prevent. You saw Storicai and the
Successor struggling by the long table. You saw the Successor snatch the hammer and deal two blows—"

The Teacher said faintly, "It was as you say."

"From this it follows that the Successor was *not*
locked in the scriptorium at the time of the slaying."
And wonder touched Ellery's voice. "Did you not tell
me that he was?"

The Teacher said, "Think, Elroï, think."

"All right, I will go back, step by step. You told me
you had locked the Successor in the scriptorium at two
o'clock because you found him dallying in the doorway
of the holy house with thoughts of a young woman, instead of being at his studies. You locked him in and retained the only key. That is the truth."

"Yea."

"But you also told me that just after the killing of Storicai in the meeting room you unlocked the door of the
scriptorium, released the Successor, and sent him out to
find me. *Un*locked the scriptorium door *after* the slaying
of the Storesman. That is the truth."

"Yea."

"But I ask myself: How is that possible? For the Successor to have been in the meeting room and to have
killed Storicai, the door to the scriptorium must have
been unlocked before the murder; yet you told me you

unlocked it after the murder . . . Ah, I see. You wished it believed that the Successor sat helpless behind a locked door between two o'clock and some time after four-twenty—to furnish the young man with an alibi that would make it impossible to suspect him of the slaying.

"Yes, I see. Just before three o'clock when you left the Holy Congregation House to visit the Slave, you unlocked the door of the scriptorium and reminded the Successor about repairing the table leg. And this time you left the scriptorium door unlocked."

The Teacher closed his eyes. "It is so."

"I did not ask you of this, therefore you did not tell me of it."

The Teacher nodded.

"But you knew I would ask other questions, and you could answer those questions only with the truth. So, Teacher, the first thing you did after realizing that Storicai was dead—just after four-twenty—was to send the Successor back into the scriptorium and lock him in— for the second time. This you did so that you could tell me truthfully that just after four-twenty you unlocked the scriptorium door, released the Successor, and sent him out to seek me. By thus telling me the truth in part only, did you protect the Successor from the consequences of his guilt and point the finger of the slaying to yourself alone."

And the Teacher said, "All that you say, Elroï, is so."

Ellery began to pace the room, his irregular footsteps echoing his troubled thoughts. "I have been wondering why you should have done this, Teacher, and I am confused. Can it truly be that you, the shepherd of the clock, are willing to give up your life that the little fox with bloodstained paws should live?"

The Teacher began to speak; but he held his tongue in time, and many moments passed. Finally he said in a firm voice, "Truly," and then added in a voice not so firm, "but only in part."

Only in part . . . ? Mystified, Ellery waited for the

old man to explain his meaning. But the Teacher's silence was unbroken.

"Teacher," said Ellery wearily, facing him. "Teacher, surely there is another way? Surely you need not die? For the Successor need not die if the whole truth be told. Surely, if he were to be put on trial, the Crownsil would be merciful. For Storicai *did* commit three great sins. He *was* caught in the act of committing them by the Successor. What the Successor did was the impulsive action of a young man with a young man's lack of control. He was outraged at Storicai's sacrilege, and he seized the first object at hand, the prayer jar, and struck blindly.

"And when Storicai recovered from the blow and ran after the Successor, surely he intended the boy bodily harm?—for a man who would profane the holy house and contemplate sacrilegious acts would have no hesitation in attempting murder to keep his crimes from becoming known. So that when the boy, fighting for his life, managed to get hold of the hammer on the table and struck out with it, surely he was not a slayer at heart? In the world from which I come such a man-slayer would be defended in the court of law by the plea of self-defense, which, if successful, results in the slayer's being declared not guilty of slaying, and so is released. Surely the Crownsil will understand?"

"It is you," said the old man sadly, "who do not understand."

"No," cried Ellery, "no, I do not! Or I do, and it is you who do not! Even if the Crownsil were to find the Successor guilty, they could not pass sentence or judgment—that duty is yours alone, as Teacher. And surely it is not conceivable that you would feel obliged to condemn the boy to his death? Surely you could, and would, show mercy?—and the Crownsil would be shamed by their Teacher's compassion. The boy need not die, Teacher; and if he need not die, you need not die in his place!"

"Elroï, Elroï," murmured the old man, "what I did was not for the Successor alone."

"What do you mean?" said Ellery, staring.

"The Slave did not request my presence in his house yesterday merely because he was ill, ill though he was. He had urgent tidings for me, for my ear alone . . . Where shall I begin?

"At the place where we first met, and you and I and the Storesman—I shall begin there. It was only last year that Storicai began to accompany me to the End-of-the-World Store. This was a great mistake, and it was mine alone. For I discovered that Storicai was a weak and covetous man. While he knew only our Valley and the things of our Valley, while he was surrounded by our simple abundance and had charge over all of it, his covetousness was not apparent. And when he knew only me, his weakness was supported.

"But at the store of Otto Schmidt he saw for the first time a box that talks, flashing jewelry, handsome cloth the like of which we do not have, succulent foods that made his mouth water—he saw wondrous things he had never known existed. And in his weakness Storicai could not resist the desire to possess them."

And Ellery, recalling the Storesman's wonder at the Duesenberg, his childish delight in the gold wrist watch, saw the man as the Teacher must have come to see him.

"I should not have allowed him to continue accompanying me to the End-of-the-World Store," the patriarch went on strongly. "But I did not then know the depth of his covetousness. No, he was careful not to betray to me the greed that was growing within him, enticing and deceiving him. He did not tell me of his greed—but he did tell the Crownsil."

"What!"

"He worked upon them behind my back. He told them of these wondrous things. At first they were incredulous. Then they were merely doubtful. And soon they began to believe. For some of the elders still dimly remembered the world outside Quenan, the things they had enjoyed as children, and when they added their memories to Storicai's tales, the younger people could not help but believe. And Storicai continued to tempt them, and in time all began to covet the things the Storesman coveted."

Ellery muttered, "Even . . . ?"

The Teacher read Ellery's mind. "Even the Weaver," he nodded in a sort of pain. "Yea, even she—though she told herself that she coveted for my sake, not her own, as women will. She wanted me, before I ceased, to partake of the wonders of which Storicai spoke so cunningly. As if I have need of such baubles and gratifications! As if I would gainsay the whole meaning of my life and the life of Quenan!"

It was the first time Ellery had ever heard the old man raise his voice, seen his eyes flash with the fires of anger. But then the fires damped, and when he spoke his voice was calm again.

"What you must understand, Elroï, is that Storicai found out he could, as punishment, be deposed. In his was craven also. He feared to do alone what he must do in order to satisfy his mean hungers, for if he were cunning he saw that if he could persuade the others of the Crownsil to join with him, he would be safe. So with his mouth smoother than oil he set out about persuading them. They had only to join with him, he said, and he would do what had to be done. He would divide the wondrous things with all in Quenan, he said, but the Crownsil would receive greater shares because of their high position. What, compared to this, was the wearing of horn buttons?"

"The Crownsil was corrupted," muttered Ellery. "The whole Crownsil!"

"The whole Crownsil—but one," the old man whispered. "The whole Crownsil—but one . . . And Storicai proceeded with his plan, and stole the key from my chamber, and made a duplicate key to the forbidden room—for the purpose of it all was, as you saw, to steal the silver dollars with which he proposed to buy the useless things he craved.

"Therefore, Elroï," and his voice became strong and steady again, "all the while I was saying to you that there was no crime in Quenan, there was crime in Quenan and I did not know it. All the while I declared that none in Quenan coveted that which was not his, my most beloved brothers and sisters were coveting, and planning to steal, and to sanction stealing, and to transgress the law and deny the Wor'd; and I did not know it.

"The Slave alone of the Crownsil of Twelve had never entered into Storicai's evil compact. Though sore of heart, he had kept silent, praying that the others would see in time the great sin they intended, and would repent and stay the hand of Storicai. But when he fell sick to dying, and they repented not, the Slave sent for me and disclosed all he knew . . . I walked back from the Slave's house with feet that walked of themselves. I had no thoughts, no feelings; I walked in blackness.

"And I entered this holy house, and I saw the Successor struggling with Storicai and snatching up the hammer to defend himself—for he is only a boy, and Storicai was a powerful man—and slay him, and I was too late to stay the great trouble of Quenan. And I saw also, as in a vision, what I must do.

"I am old, Elroï, and the days allotted to me cannot be many more. The Successor has been reared to take my place since his first breath, for this is our way. He was not ever of the conspiracy, remember; that was only among the Crownsil. He was outraged by what he saw Storicai trying to do, and his only thought was to keep the holy treasure intact, and see the Storesman punished.

"He has the leaping blood of youth, Elroï, but he believes with all his soul in the Wor'd; he will gain wisdom as his blood cools and he will spend his life faithfully, as I have spent mine, to be the Teacher of our people. And, in any case, there is none trained to take his place."

The old man had raised himself to a sitting position in his earnestness. "All these things went through my mind in an instant. And I knew the Successor must remain unstained in the eyes of the community, if he is to command their utter belief and trust. Therefore I take his sin upon myself and depart from them."

The wind spoke to the trees and the frogs spoke to the wind; but in the dim chamber neither spoke.

Until Ellery said, "Teacher, I cannot approve of it. Even in your own terms I condemn it. You once said to me that we must seek the truth, that the truth will save us—"

The old man nodded, unperturbed. "For thus it is written," he said. And Ellery wondered, not for the first time, if the Teacher meant *Thus the truth is written,* or *Thus it must be.*

"How can we seek the truth, and how can the truth save us, if we act out a lie?" Then he burst out: "What evil have you done, that you should sacrifice your life?"

Some measure of the old man's tranquillity left him; he uttered a sigh that seemed to come from great depths.

"You are mistaken, Elroï. I have done great evil indeed. For if the Crownsil have sinned, then have I not sinned more? Is it not I who has been their Teacher? Their sins are upon my head; their guilt, that cuts into my heart, is my own.

"It is not they who have failed me; it is I who have failed them. Or they could not have done this thing.

"And as I am their Teacher still, so I must teach them now—since the teaching of my words has failed —by the teaching of my example. And the example is that I shall take their sin upon myself. For if faith in the Wor'd is lost, then all is lost, and Quenan becomes as the outside from which we fled . . . nay, worse, for my people have had no experience with sin, and in the outside they would be as sheep without the shepherd when snow shuts out the sky. I love them, Elroï, and how better can I show my love?—if only they love each other. It must be done."

But Ellery mumbled, "I will tell them the truth."

And the Teacher smiled and asked the ancient question, "What is truth? Today at the trial you told them what you then held to be the truth, and they believed you. And now you wish to tell them the contrary, so that they may believe the contrary. Do you think they will?"

The old man drew a deep breath; his spare body was

taken with a shudder, quickly suppressed. "If you tell them the truth, Elroï, I will deny it. I will deny it, and they will believe me as they have always believed me. And what will you have gained?"

Ellery beat his fist into his palm. "You know you will not and cannot deny the truth. You know you will not and cannot ever lie to them!"

The old man trembled. "Then do not, I pray you, force me to lie to them after seven decades. But," and he raised his voice, not in agitation but in emphasis, "but I would do so, Elroï, for it is written that I am doing that which must be done, that which was ordained of old for the end of days. You have been the instrument prophesied, and my love for you is great; but some things I know better than you, for all your knowledge. If you have love for me, then I pray you do not tell them. Believe in me."

Ellery sat, immobilized. What to do, what to do? Rush headlong to his car, speed off to find . . . whom? the police? the sheriff? the governor? the Army?—someone, anyone who would keep tomorrow's human sacrifice from being made? And yet, to do that would be to expose Quenan to a world that could only destroy the Valley. But it was destroyed already. Or was it? The Teacher was prepared to give his life in the belief that it was not. Who was he to set his small judgment against the towering spirit of this old man?

And, as Ellery sat, treacherously it came stealing over him again, that strange, utter fatigue. It began to make a roaring in his ears.

What to do? *What to do?*

The old man spoke gently. "In that cabinet is bread, and also wine, and it is late," he said. "Will you sup with me?"

Ellery shut the door of the old man's room quietly behind and simply stood there. In the meeting hall the single lamp cast its dim glow. Once it had seemed golden, but no longer. It came to his exhausted mind that he was waiting for something. But what?

He pressed his palms against his eyes. Curious patterns were shifting kaleidoscopically. Suddenly they formed a face. He felt immediate relief, and took away the shielding hands, and crossed the room to the door of the scriptorium. He knocked, and there was no answer. He tried the door; it was unlocked, and he went in. The scriptorium was empty. Of course. The Successor's bedchamber. He switched on his flashlight and went to the other door and knocked and, again, there was no answer. He opened the door; the Successor was gone. Mechanically he retreated to the long hall.

He heard himself groan. Every atom in his body seemed to be crying out for rest, and the distance to his own room stretched infinitely. The bench beckoned, and he decided to sit down.

His legs had already begun to undertake the labor of getting to the bench when a peculiar sound from outdoors paralyzed them. In the same instant the face, which had vanished, sprang again into his mind's eye. So he made his way painfully out of the Holy Congregation House. He paused outside the door.

There was something in the darkness that made noises like an owl's noises, or a child's; but this thing that he barely saw was not an owl, was too large to be a child, and yet was not shaped like a man.

Ellery's parts shrank in upon themselves.

He took himself in hand. On legs as taut and tingling as they had been leaden-weighted, he approached the thing in the night. Not until later did it occur to him that he could have used his flashlight, which he clutched throughout.

Glimmer—faint in the faint starlight. Bulk—close to the ground, cool and damp. Whimper—incoherent, alien. And then a cough, and then a sob.

Fear dropped from Ellery like melting ice, and he knelt and touched what lay there, and moved his hand over it. It was a man clad in a robe, doubled up, hands so tightly pressed against his face that Ellery had to use all his enfeebled strength to dislodge them. He felt a beard rimming the jaw, the soft curling beard of youth.

The Successor.

There was a whispering in the darkness.

Ellery bent closer, trying to make it out. ". . . *tell them, tell them, tell them.*"

"I cannot," a second voice said, the Successor's. Whose, then, had been the whisper? The young man's eyes were open now, holes of darkness in his face. "I cannot tell them," he said.

Ellery tried to rise, staggered. The Successor looked startled; instinctively he put forth a supporting hand, and they struggled together to their feet.

"Why were you crying?" Ellery said.

"You said, Elroï, that I must tell the Crownsil and the people the true happenings," the Successor whispered. "But . . ."

That was when Ellery remembered the flashlight. He switched it on and set it down on the ground so that it reflected from a large pale rock. The boy's face was masklike; to see his lips move was a shock.

"But?"

"But I cannot say the truth. I do not dare."

So it came about that Ellery found himself sitting on the cold ground trying to develop a Socratic dialogue with the boyish man-slayer. In the first place, he asked, once the Crownsil had been made to understand the circumstances of the crime, was it likely they would again convict? But even if they were to convict, was it likely the Teacher would pronounce the dread sentence a second time? But even were the Teacher to pronounce sentence against him, was there reason for the Successor to submit? He was a boy, he had a long lifetime before him: could he not flee? Who was there in Quenan to restrain him by force? Nor need he feel afraid to face the unknown world. Ellery would be to him as a brother, as an elder brother.

But—"I cannot, I do not dare."

Cannot, do not dare? When the alternative is the death of the Teacher? Canst thou remain silent, *darest* thou?

"Can you watch a man like your Teacher go to his death for a crime which, in the first place, he did not commit and, in the second place, was not a crime but an act of self-defense? If you're worthy to be the Successor," Ellery said, "you will speak out!"

The mask before him was the mask of tragedy. The change wrought in the short time since he had last seen the boy was horrifying. The eyes were cloudy and deep-sunken, the bloodless lips down-twisted, twitching; the whole young head seemed skeletal.

"You do not understand, Elroï." The Successor's voice, the Teacher's words.

"Then make me understand! Because otherwise I will have no choice but to bring in authorities from the outside world to save your Teacher's life. And that will mean the end of Quenan."

Over and over again, the boy wrung his hands. "I know everything you have told me," he cried. "I would do as you ask—oh, Elroï, you would not have to ask! But I am helpless. Why do you think I remained silent at the trial? I could not speak because the Teacher forbade it! He forbids it still, and I dare not disobey him."

"Why, Successor? *Why* can't you disobey him? What would happen to you if you did?" Ellery demanded.

The young head rolled from side to side in agony. "I do not know what would happen, Elroï. It does not matter what would happen. It is as if you were to ask me, What would happen were you to raise your arms and fly to the stars? You do not understand, I cannot do it. I have never in my life disobeyed the Teacher and I cannot disobey him now!"

Ellery stared at the tragic mask, and suddenly he understood. The Successor was like the next-to-last Emperor of China, the nephew of the wicked Empress Dowager, imprisoned at her command when he tried to reform the corrupt practices of her regency. In prison he was visited by officials secretly in sympathy with his cause. Let the Son of Heaven but give the word, they said, and loyal troops would liberate him and place the "Old Buddha" herself in confinement. But the Emperor shook his head. It was impossible, he said. How could one raise one's hand against a venerable ancestor? And he died a prisoner still, held fast by bars far stronger than the bars of his cell.

I cannot do it. I cannot disobey him.

The words rang in Ellery's ears until they filled the night.

He remembered the dark lane flowing past him. He remembered the path moving like water under his feet. He remembered the noise in his ears, like a howling wind.

But he did not remember stumbling to his pallet and falling on it; he did not remember the new dawn creeping up from behind Crucible Hill.

He knew only darkness.

VI

FRIDAY

April 7.

WHEN HE OPENED his eyes there were no shadows, but the great hush that hung over the Valley was not the usual noontime quiet. It was the silence of a ghost town, or rather of a town or a *Mary Celeste* suddenly abandoned by its human beings.

Then an ass brayed, and another; a bellow burst from the chest of a bull; dogs began to howl, as if something dreadful were about to happen.

Or was happening.

Or had happened? With a cry, Ellery jumped out of bed. But then he remembered. It was not to be until sundown.

But . . . the silence? Had all Quenan fled into the desert rather than stay to witness?

He was still in his stale and rumpled clothes. The sleep had not refreshed him; and the sun pouring through the window did not wash away the ache in his bones.

He went out into the lane. No one was in sight, and he walked through the village. Here and there, through an open window, he caught a glimpse of movement; once he saw a distant someone—the Waterman?—working in a field. *The mills are to turn, and the dry fields burn.* No, the people of Quenan had not left their Valley. They simply could not bear to look upon it on this day, as if the hills themselves were due to depart with the departing sun. Most of them had withdrawn into their houses and shut the doors.

Great must be their grief.

And great was the silence which hung over the Valley of the Shadow, and all that endless afternoon Ellery wrestled with his problem and found no answer to it.

The choices always seemed to come down to three:

He could let the events take their course, bowing to the will of the Teacher.

He could tell the truth to the community. But in that case, the Teacher had said, he would deny it, and the people would believe him and not Ellery; and Ellery knew that this was so.

He could go for help to prevent the sentence's being carried out. But then Quenan itself would die.

Talk about Hobson!

Ellery walked the tree-lined lanes, climbed the green terrace of the hills, picked his way along the immaculate furrows of the fields. No one appeared to speak or even wave to him. Twice he headed in the direction of the only figures he laid eyes on in his wanderings, but when he reached the place no one was there. He could not bring himself to knock on any door.

Late in the afternoon he found himself drawn back to the Holy Congregation House. The Teacher was alone there, sitting on a stool. He greeted Ellery with the familiar gesture of benediction and indicated the bench. Ellery sank onto it. The old man seemed completely at peace.

"Teacher," said Ellery, "I beg you to reconsider."

"Very well," the patriarch said calmly.

Ellery's heart jumped. "Then you will tell them the truth?" he cried.

For a moment the old man said nothing; then: "I

have reconsidered, Elroï, as you asked. I find no reason to change that which is written. I will say no more to the people, nor will you."

The sun began to set. The people seemed to come from everywhere—houses, barns, fields, trees, shadows —springing up like the reapings of the dragon's teeth. They came from everywhere and became one, a sluggish beast of many heads sluggishly moving along.

And Ellery became one with them.

He saw the Teacher, tall among the many, the throng making way for him with sighs and moans as he moved slowly through, his right hand describing the ritual blessing.

And so Quenan came to the place; and when the crowds parted and Ellery saw what it was that their bodies had concealed, lying on the earth, he almost cried out with relief and joy.

How could he have been so blind as to take literally what was intended as a symbol only? What he was witnessing was a parallel to the rites of the Penitentes of the New Mexico mountains—the Brotherhood of the Light, as they called themselves—who yearly re-enacted the great passion of their religion and chose one of their number for the central role. Performed in secret places, intended as a purging of sin, the mystery stopped short of the taking of life, although its principal suffered torments enough.

He wondered how the isolated community of Quenan had learned of these remarkable rites. Or had they developed a similar rite independently, altering, as it were, the ancient prompt-book? For what he was now witnessing . . .

The Teacher lay down in the place prepared for him. There was now not even a sigh.

So might the ancient Egyptians have stood at the annual re-enactment of the death of Osiris—knowing it was drama, yet not-knowing, too, with one part of themselves believing it to be a real thing, happening before their eyes.

And the Superintendent stepped forth from among them, holding a vessel of some sort in his cupped hands. And all breath was stopped, even the breath of the wind.

The Superintendent tenderly lifted the Teacher's head with his left hand, and held the vessel to the ancient lips with his right, and then departed from him. The Teacher lay perfectly still. The sun set then, plunging the scene in blood, reddening the palms of the recumbent patriarch. All at once a soft spring breeze arose, and the grasses whispered in alarm . . .

Ellery awoke to a great anger. To allow himself to be so cozened and bewitched! The Teacher and his puppets had succeeded in infecting him with the disease of their fantasies, making him believe that the real was unreal and the unreal real. But he was cured. What had seemed an experience of pathos and profound tragedy was simply a distasteful demonstration of bumpkin fanaticism. The old man was a natural-born actor, and soon the lesser actors in this primitive drama would be stepping forward to perform their silly roles, too. Well, he had had enough of the nonsense! It was time to call a halt.

A woman nearby began to wail, rocking back and forth. Another woman—ah, the Weaver!—took up the lament. The children began to cry in a frightened way. (They had been coached, too!) And then the man . . .

Ellery raised his arms high and shouted, "This has gone far enough!" and strode over to where the old man lay with arms outstretched to the darkening skies; and Ellery dropped to one knee, and reached out his hand to shake the thin shoulder.

But the hand remained in midair.

Out of the jumble in Ellery's head an orderly thought took shape: I have been following the wrong prompt-book, too. The laws of Quenan are not the laws of Rome. The drink was not the symbolic preliminary to carrying out the symbolic sentence; it *was* the sentence, and there was nothing symbolic about it.

The Teacher had not been acting after all. His face was at peace still, but it was not the same peace; in the manner prescribed by the laws of Quenan—as it was written that it must be, and as it was done, feet together, arms outstretched, in holy symmetry—the Teacher lay dead.

VII

SATURDAY

April 8.

AND ELLERY WEPT.

VIII

SUNDAY

April 9.

THE DAY WAS well along when Ellery left the house he had occupied during his stay in Quenan. The day before, he had not left it at all. Now, standing on the door-sill and looking about, though the flowers still bloomed and the leaves hung green he felt even more strongly that this was a place of the dead. Not a soul was to be seen, not a sound to be heard. He stepped out into the lane

The public buildings, as he passed, seemed hollow ruins; the little houses, earth-stained artifacts of a long-crumbled past. It was just as well, he thought, that the people had crept into their holes. It meant that he didn't have to say good-bye to anyone (and suppose one of them raised a hand in blessing and said, "The Wor'd go with you"?—it would be too much to bear). No, it was time to go, and the sooner and more quietly the better. A week and a day "out of time, out of space" were enough for a mere mortal.

Still, as Ellery strolled through the silent hamlet, he could not help remembering with pleasure the previous strolls, the open faces of the Quenanites, the brown-skinned children offering him flowers shyly . . . Here loomed a tree he had grown fond of, there shone a familiar splotch of ochre on a wall. Had it been a mere week or so that he had been here? It felt more as if in his own flesh he had made the trek across the burning sands with the founding fathers of Quenan.

He came for the last time to the Holy Congregation House. There hung the bell, unmoved. He scanned the familiar legend on it:

> *From Earth's gross ores my Tongue's set free*
> *To sound the Hours upon the Sea*

Yes, the hills walling Quenan, together with the Valley, might be likened to a ship, the surrounding desert the sea—a ship forever becalmed under a cloudless sky, yet always with some creak of calamity impending.

Should he go into the holy house? The Teacher was not there. Why bother? Yet the Teacher *was* there. He was in every crack and cranny. Well, why not bid farewell to a ghost?

Ellery went in.

The holy house seemed empty, although the Successor must be in his chambers. The Successor? He had already succeeded! The Teacher was dead; long live the Teacher. What thoughts must be going through the boy's mind? And what must he be feeling? Grief? Guilt? Remorse? Terror? Well, whatever they were, he would have to wrestle with them alone.

Through the silent conventicle he went, and paused at the door of the forbidden room. He turned, not realizing at first that he was looking for the old man to ask permission to enter. Almost he sensed the prophet's presence. But only almost. He turned back to the door. The sense of violation, of desecration, was still strong, and he had to force himself to try the door. It was unlocked (*O tempora! O mores!*), and he went in.

Nothing was changed in the sanquetum. The eternal lamp still burned; how, being eternal, could it not? And the silence was here as always. The light thinned and thickened, thinned and thickened; but then the shadows which had been set to dancing by the opening of the door settled down; and all at once Ellery had the most absurd feeling that the old Teacher was with him in the little room, not merely in spirit but in body also . . . and the rich voice, blessing him . . .

He shook himself back to reality (and *now* what was real?) and stared into the old glass-front china closet, the "arque" the old man had bought to house the mysterious "book which was lost." On its top shelf still stood the two columns of coins, fifteen Carson City dollars in one, fifteen Carson City dollars in the other . . . thirty pieces of silver indeed. The old Teacher's father could hardly have dreamed, when he accepted the store of silver dollars to become a treasure for Quenan, that he was enshrining a curse. A curse that would lie silently, "hidden in the urn," for seventy years, and then unloose a passion that would doom his begotten son.

Ellery almost reached out to steal those terrible coins and scatter them in the desert.

But he could not bring himself to touch them.

But the book, the open book on the lower shelf in its black-letter German type—that was something else. About the book he would have to take action, fitting action, or he would never sleep soundly again.

He opened the glass door of the arque and lifted the volume out as if it were alive. He could not run the risk of letting someone—the Successor; no, the new Teacher —see him taking it away; so he tucked it under one arm securely between his shirt and his jacket, and buttoned the jacket, and felt the book burn his flesh. And he left the sanquetum forever.

He was about to shut the sanquetum door when a great thought struck him. Why not leave it open? *Fiat Lux . . . Mehr Licht!* Let the shadows die.

He left it open.

For the last time he made the trip back to his house, packed the book in his grip, and closed his luggage. And so farewell. He had been received almost as a god. There was no reason to assume that he was now held in less reverence; probably he was held in more, since awe and terror had been added. The instrument of the fulfillment of a prophecy, he had helped destroy something tender and potent and unique. Quenan might still look up to him; but it could hardly be with love.

His lips tightened as he snapped the lock on his suitcase and left.

He looked around to get his bearings. There—up that path, behind the vines. That was the way he had come down with an ageless ancient clasping a trumpet beneath his robe.

Ellery climbed the hill slowly, from time to time glancing down the inner slope. No one was in sight. No, there was one. On the farther slope, among the stones that marked the peaceful place, a misshapen little figure crept. Ellery shuddered and went on.

One last time he looked back. The grays and browns had now become a blur of dun, almost colorless.

And then he reached the crest of the hill and passed over it. The Valley of Quenan (Canaan? Kenan? What? He would probably never know now), the whole incredible site, vanished from view.

He had to laugh.

He had gone down the rocky face of the hill, trudged through the sands to his car, tossed his bags in, got behind the wheel, turned on the ignition—and nothing.

The battery was dead.

O Pioneers, ye knew not the blessings of the motorcar.

The water in his radiator had evaporated, too. That was easily remedied (easily?): he had only to go back to the village. But the battery? Dead. He looked around. Everything was dead—the desert, the hill. Nothing lived anywhere; no breath stirred; the air lay panting on the corpse, disconsolate.

Otto Schmidt sold gas, so he possibly had a battery

around, or at least a booster. But how to get to Schmidt's store? It would be a long walk in the desert; too chancy. Have to borrow a donkey from the village . . .

But first, the book.

Ellery dug it out of his bag.

He went off a little from the car and laid the book on the sand and began to scoop out a shallow hole with his naked fingers. The sand was powdery, and he had no trouble. Then he began tearing pages from the book, crumpling each one and tossing it into the hole. When the hollow was almost full he struck a match and dropped it in.

In the beginning he knew the paper was on fire only from the magic spread of char. But then the flames came.

Ellery watched them with a wholly new savagery of satisfaction. From time to time he crumpled more pages and flung them into the heart of the flames.

At last nothing was left of the book but its cover.

He stared at the words printed on it in black-letter German and, in spite of the heat, he shivered. In all the long history of written communication, had there ever been a sadder misreading than the old Teacher's of this book? He had wanted so fervently to believe in the existence of the legendary "lost" book of Quenan. And then the patriarch had gone into the End-of-the-World Store one day for supplies, and there on the counter had lain a book, and on its cover he had seen three words in archaic-looking lettering, in a strange language that he could not read; but the three words lay one under another, so that their first letters were lined up vertically; and he had read the acrostic:

𝕸

𝕽

𝕳

How the old man's heart must have pounded! It was a wonder that it had not stopped altogether. For the "lost" book was said to have been entitled Mk'n, or

which was a difference of only one letter, and the difference was so small in appearance—and who knew, he must have thought, but that the title as handed down, Mk'n, might not originally have been Mk'h, and corrupted somewhere along the route of time?

He had wanted to believe that this was the sacred book of Quenan; and so he had believed.

And how, Ellery thought, how could I have told him that he was selling his faith of peace and brotherhood for a mess of carnage?

He gathered some twigs from a nearby bush, and he carefully ignited them, and when they were burning brightly he laid the cover on them. It caught fire; and the flames took on an evil look, as if the fire itself were corrupted by what it was consuming.

The title seemed to have a demon life of its own. Even as the cover turned to ash, the title clung to its vile substance, standing out clearly, almost coldly in the flames:

**Mein
Kampf
Hitler**

And then it, too, gave up its twisting form and died. And Ellery ground its ashes under his heel.

He had taken only a few steps back toward the Valley when he heard a rumble in the sky that grew steadily to a roar. Queer! The Potter (had it been the Potter?—it now seemed so long ago) had remarked on the increasing number of aircraft passing through Quenan's skies, yet during his entire stay Ellery had not seen or heard one.

He stopped to scan the sky, and—yes!—there it was. A small single-seater plane, not a fighter or any military plane he knew of, was coming toward him from the south. Ellery watched it with growing anxiety. The roar was becoming irregular, erratic . . . staccato . . . and then there was an explosion and a burst of fire and in an instant the little aircraft was one great flame and the flame was flashing and tumbling as it passed almost directly overhead.

My God, the Valley, Ellery thought; if it should hit Quenan . . . ! But he saw that it was going to crash on the slope of Crucible Hill facing the desert, falling just short of the village. And in the same thankful moment a parachute blossomed above him. Ellery began to run.

He saw the parachutist hit the sands only a short way off. For an instant the man lay still, as if stunned; but by the time Ellery reached him he was on his feet, tugging at the silk, unbuckling himself.

"Are you all right?" Ellery cried.

The man looked up from his harness. He smiled and said, "Just fine, *amigo.*"

Ellery blinked. The voice was deep and strong, and yet it had a gentle quality; it sounded familiar. But it was not so much the voice. The flyer was a young man, tall and slender and dark, with curly black hair and aquiline features, quite handsome in an odd way; although he had obviously shaved that morning, his gaunt cheeks showed the foreshadows of a heavy beard. I've seen this fellow somewhere, Ellery thought; he certainly looks as familiar as he sounds. And then he stood very still, in the wash of an icy wave. The young man looked like . . . looked like . . .

Ellery shook his head, feeling foolish. Yet it was true. The young man looked as the Teacher must have looked when he was thirty years old.

"Talk about luck," the stranger said, stepping out of the harness. "Imagine conking out over the desert and coming down at the feet of a Good Samaritan with a car."

"Not such a Good Samaritan, I'm afraid," Ellery said. "My battery's dead."

The stranger smiled again. "We'll make out," he said. "Don't worry about it."

"All right," Ellery said, smiling back. "I won't." As they began to walk slowly toward the car, he asked, "Where were you heading?"

"North—up Pyramid Lake way," the young man said. "Crop-dusting. I'm a C.O., you know."

"C.O.? The only thing that means to me is 'Commanding Officer.'"

"Hardly," and the stranger laughed.

"Oh," Ellery said. "You mean a conscientious objector."

"Yes." He said it quite calmly—quite, Ellery thought, as the old Teacher might have said it; and smiled faintly at his fantasy. "I got an agricultural deferment. The funny part of it is, I learned to fly in the cadet program. I was on the wild side, I'm afraid. Rich father, plenty of money, out for thrills and kicks. Then one day a buddy of mine had the same thing happen to him that just happened to me. Only he didn't get to bail out."

"I see."

"I saw, too. For the first time, I guess. And I began to think—you know, man and God, man and fellow-man, man and his eternal soul, all that. Well, I hauled myself out of the cadet program and began to read and study. Found myself after a while. And knew one thing for sure—no killing for me. I wrestled with *that* one for a long, long time. But that's the way it is. I couldn't do it. No matter how they tag me."

"It must be rough," Ellery said.

"Not so rough," the young stranger said. "Not if you know why you're doing it. You find yourself, and you live by what you find. That's why I don't think I'll keep on with this job after the war is over. I've been thinking of social work of some kind. Well, we'll see." They had reached the car, and the stranger opened the hood and poked around. "Dead, all right. Any idea where the nearest town is? Say!" He had straightened up and was staring at the nearby hill. "Look at that."

Ellery looked. And he saw on the ridge of Crucible Hill, in a long line of black figures against the sky, like paper cutouts, the people of Quenan. And it suddenly came to him what had happened, and the icy wave washed over him once more. They had heard the coughing death of the plane, run out of their houses and seen it come down in a streak of flame from the sky. *Like a burning chariot . . . like a chariot of fire . . .*

They had seen the man fall from the burning plane. *No. They had seen the man descend from out the ineffable heavens.*

And they had come to him.

"May I ask your name?" Ellery murmured.

"What? Oh." The young stranger kept staring at the people. "Manuel—"

And they shall call his name Emmanuel . . . Ellery felt a quiver ripple through him. His knees actually began to tremble. I won't fall down, he told himself fiercely, I won't; it's weakness, the awful fatigue I've been gripped by . . .

"—Aquina," the young man finished.

It's too much, the other Ellery insisted wildly in his head—too much, too much, too much; it's more than reason can bear. *Aquina, Quenan.* Too much, an infinite complexity beyond the grasp of man. Acknowledge. Acknowledge and depart.

"Those people on the ridge," Manuel Aquina said in a slow, not-quite-puzzled way. "Is there a town beyond that hill?"

The setting sun touched the strange young eyes, and they began to blaze.

"There is a new world beyond that hill," Ellery heard a slow, not-quite-puzzled voice respond—his own? "And I think . . . I think . . . its people wait for you."